DESIRE

CRUZ & LOGAN

A.D. ELLIS

ONE
CRUZ ADAMS

A VIOLENT SHATTERING of glass rang through the air and I didn't even think. With a quick command to a customer in line for them to call the police, I rushed from my newly appointed spot as the doorman at the Wishing Well bar and ran toward the alley. Grunts, groans, and savage sounds of fists meeting bone greeted me.

As the adopted Mexican child of white parents growing up near a dangerous city, I'd been lucky to avoid gangs during my teen years. That luck had run out when I got out of private Catholic high school and ended up in the wrong place, at the wrong time, with the wrong friends, and no money for a good lawyer.

Being on the periphery of gangs and spending five years in prison had seasoned me to physical assault.

Maybe I'd gone soft in my thirty-five years, but I wasn't prepared to find the slim, frail young man being beaten in the alleyway.

Remington was a fairly quiet town. Compared to the places I'd spent the past eight years, it was a mecca of peaceful solitude and welcoming, supportive friends. My new boss at the local auto shop, Jesse Thompson—he'd also gotten me the job at the Wishing Well—said there wasn't much violence in the area.

So, finding two men beating the shit out of what looked to be a kid took me by surprise and had my blood boiling. The young man had dropped to the ground, curled in a fetal position, as they kicked and punched at him, the remnants of a broken bottle dully reflecting the dim alley light.

"Get the fuck off him." I grabbed a piece from a broken wooden pallet leaning against the concrete wall. I hadn't been in a physical altercation since before prison, and very few even then, but I barreled into the melee ready to kick some ass.

The two men paused in their attack and backed away, hands up.

Putting myself between them and the guy on the ground—who was moaning, so I at least knew he was alive—I held up the jagged piece of wood and sent up a silent prayer that the police would arrive soon. Doing my best to make a mental note of the men's clothing and physical features, I willed the kid writhing on the ground to be okay.

When the sirens blared, blue and red lights flashing around the alleyway, I glanced quickly over my shoulder to see two officers arriving. They approached slowly, taking in the scene as they moved closer.

The morons in front of me squawked and fled, scrambling up the chain link fence and falling hard on the other side. Grunting and groaning in pain, they lurched to their feet and encouraged each other to run as they limped into the darkness.

One officer took off toward the patrol car while the other handed me his card. "We'll need your statement and his if he wants to press charges. Call for an ambulance," he ordered before joining his partner. They sped off in pursuit of the two attackers.

"No hospital," the kid on the ground moaned. "Please."

I tossed my makeshift weapon aside and dropped to my knees next to him just as Jesse poked his head out the back door.

"Holy shit, what happened? You need help? Did you call 9-1-1?" Jesse asked as he stepped into the alley beside me.

"No, no ambulance. No hospital, I'm fine," the

kid grunted as he rolled to a sitting position and reached for a worn backpack a few feet away.

"You were kicked and punched several times," I said, "you may have internal injuries. You should let a doctor check you out."

"No, can't go to the hospital. I've been hurt worse. Protected my head, face, and ribs. Arms and legs heal pretty easy. I'm fine." He lifted his head as if it weighed a thousand pounds and gave a weak smile.

"What happened?" Jesse asked.

"The one guy offered me twenty bucks for a blow job and was all for it until his buddy showed up. They both went off on me, then you showed up." He smiled at me again, a bit stronger this time. "Thank you for stopping them. Wasn't a situation I was sure I'd get out of if you hadn't come along." He shrugged and his face clouded. "Been in a lot worse, but not for a while. Took me by surprise."

"You got a place to stay?" I asked, taking in his dirty clothes and generally unkempt appearance. "Someone to take care of those injuries?" I knew from my past that if a person was that adamant about not going to the hospital, there was likely a reason and no amount of arguing would change their mind.

"I'll be fine. Could I maybe use the restroom in

there? Wash up and get some water?" The kid pointed to the back door of the bar. "I won't take long, I promise."

I glanced at Jesse who shook his head.

The kid's shoulders drooped. "No problem, I get it. Thanks again for your help."

Jesse cleared his throat. "Take him to Bev," he said quietly. "If the police come back, I'll give them your number and tell them what I know." He gave a nod before walking back into the bar.

"Look, I'm not going to force you to go to the hospital, but I can't let you go off on your own. I've got a room..."

"Sorry, man. Most nights, I'd be up for it if it meant some money in my pocket, but my whole body is throbbing, definitely not sucking dick or bending over tonight." He laughed bitterly as he struggled to stand.

It took me a moment to wrap my head around what he was saying. "What? Fuck, no. I'm not asking you for sex. Fuck, kid. What type of person do you take me for?"

He looked me up and down and shrugged, his eyes tired and his body sagging. "Most guys I know wouldn't care as long as they had somewhere to shove their dick. You seem nice enough, I'll give you a rain check, yeah? I can come back when I'm feeling better; not gonna lie, I could use the money."

Holy fucking shit.

I ran a hand over my face. "Look, kid."

He snarled, "I'm not a kid. Be twenty-one soon. Probably done more shit in life than you could even dream of."

I scoffed. "You spend five years in prison just for being poor and caught up with the wrong crowd?"

He narrowed his eyes and lifted his chin. "No. You lose your parents, bounce around foster care, and end up living with a woman who pimped you out to every willing dick she could find?"

My gut roiled and I closed my eyes. "Sounds like we've both got some shitty pasts. Look, I'm not asking for sex," I huffed. "I rent a room at this really nice house with this amazing old lady…"

He bristled.

"Not like that. She's like a grandma. There are seven renters there. At least let me get you some food and have one of my roommates who's an EMT check you out." I wanted to promise a hot shower and place to sleep as well, but he looked ready to bolt so I stopped with the food for the moment.

"I'm supposed to believe that you want to take me home just to feed me and make sure I'm not too banged up?" He wrapped long, thin arms around his slim torso.

I gave a curt nod. "I've got a record, yeah, but I'm not a bad guy. Been out eight years. Not so much as even a speeding ticket since then. That guy that came out here? He hired me at his auto repair shop—ran a background check. This bar hired me—they ran a check, too. Hell, even the lady I rent from ran one and checked in with my old parole officer." I stood and held my hands out in front of me. "If you won't let me get you to a hospital, at least let me get you some food and bandaged up."

The kid looked like he was about to fall over, but he was fighting with himself to say no.

"My name is Cruz Adams. I live with some of the kindest, most caring people you'll ever meet. Let me get you some food. You don't have to make any big decisions right now. Just a warm place and food."

His eyes darted down the alley. "The shelter is full tonight. That's why I was here trying to get some money." He dropped his head. "I don't usually sell myself for money if I can help it. Shelters usually have okay food. Haven't been in Remington long, but their place is nice; just fills up fast since it's small." His stomach rumbled. "I could eat," he whispered, cheeks red in the dim streetlight as he hugged his backpack.

"Let's go then. I'll give you my phone and my license to hold onto while we drive if that makes you feel safer." I handed the kid my phone and ID, hoping to God I wasn't making a huge mistake.

He stared at the items in his hand as he followed me to my car. "Damn, that's pretty dumb, mister."

"Call me Cruz," I said. Shrugging, I continued, "Just want you to know you can trust me."

We climbed into the car and I started the engine. "Seatbelt."

"Never get in a car without putting it on," he said quietly. "My parents were killed in a car accident when I was ten. They never wore theirs so I've always figured it was what killed them."

"Sorry to hear that. I never knew my mom, other than her last name was Cruz. No idea about my father. The couple who adopted me did their best to immerse me in my Mexican heritage—something I really appreciate—and gave me the name Cruz as a remembrance to my mother." A wave of sadness washed over me. "They died when I was in prison. Mom first, she just slipped away in her sleep, and Dad the next year—I think from a broken heart. They weren't rich, but they were good people. I miss them." I glanced his way. "Sorry, that was a bit heavy." I'd barely told all of that to Bev and Jesse, why was I telling a kid I just met?

"No worries."

"You got a name?" I asked.

He started to refuse, I saw the look of rebellion cross his face, but he dropped his head against the seat and sighed. "Logan Miles."

"Nice to meet you, Logan." I pulled the car onto Pleasure Boulevard before turning right onto Remington Way. Parking in front of a large Victorian house, I gestured toward the place. "This is it."

We got out of the car and Logan giggled as he looked at the street signs on the corner. "Your address is 69069 Remington Way?"

"Yep. Remington Place at 69069 Remington Way and Pleasure Boulevard," I confirmed. "Most amazing address I've ever had the good fortune of laying my head."

"This place has to cost you a fortune," Logan muttered.

"Nah, you'd be surprised. Bev makes sure it's affordable."

"It's beautiful," Logan murmured as he took in the massive old home.

"Wait until you see inside." I led the way to the back steps and hoped Jesse had called to tell Bev we were on our way.

I'd been at Remington Place for about four months and—aside from the twenty-two years I spent with my parents—I'd never felt more loved or accepted; always wondered if Ronnie and Paula Adams would have felt the same about their precious adopted son if they'd known I was gay.

When Bev met us in the kitchen, concern marring her face, I knew bringing Logan home with me had been the right move. For some reason, I was drawn to the kid—shit, I knew he said he was almost twenty-one, so legally an adult, but he looked like he was barely eighteen and seemed much younger than my thirty-five years. Something in his eyes, though, told me he'd seen a lot—been through a lot—and I needed to stop thinking about him as a kid.

"I have Dre gathering some medical supplies. Khi is on shift or he'd help, too," she said to me before wrapping Logan in a gentle hug. "I'm Bev King and this is my home. You're safe and welcome here for as long as you need."

Wondering what Bev would think, but not sure what the other option would be, I ushered Logan toward the stairs. "He can use my room for now."

Bev gave a nod. "I think a shower is in order. Dre will be back soon with the medical supplies and I'll get some food fixed."

"Thank you, ma'am," Logan muttered, a mixture of pain, exhaustion, and too much shit in his young life evident in his quivery voice. "I won't interrupt for long, but a shower does sound amazing."

"There's no hurry here, son. You eat and rest. No rush to leave," Bev told him and gave me a look that I knew meant she was going to offer him a place to stay. The woman had been a life saver for me, and I wanted that for Logan as well. He needed a safe place to sleep and Bev had that.

In my room.

I was the last to move in which meant I'd be the last to get a roommate. But all the other rooms were full, so that left my tiny room for me and Logan to share. I wondered if one of the twin beds in the basement storage would fit or if I'd need to downsize from my queen to a twin as well.

A slight shiver of apprehension ghosted through me, but I pushed it aside. The only thing that mattered right then was that Logan had a safe place to stay.

TWO
LOGAN MILES

"You can toss your bag in here," Cruz said. "I'll grab you some clothes. I'm guessing Spencer or Rai are about your size. Give me two minutes and I'll be right back."

I watched him rush across the hall and knock on a door.

Not putting down my backpack—it held all of my worldly possessions, which admittedly wasn't much —I took in the room. I'd heard Cruz say it was his room and I could use it. A shiver ran through me and a knot formed in my stomach as I took in the queen bed. Would he expect me to fuck him for a place to sleep?

Stop. He already assured you he wasn't looking for sex. Is there anything about that man that seems creepy?

No, there really wasn't. I'd been used and abused by men, and a few women, for much of my life. I had a sixth sense about people—maybe I'd always had it, maybe it was honed during the years I was trafficked by Lilly.

Fuck. I hated thinking about her, wanted to forget she'd ever existed, wanted to forget the horror she'd put me through. At first, I'd thought she was my ticket out of the hell-hole of foster homes—I'd not been the most cooperative or well-behaved kid at school or in the temporary homes and it showed in the way I was treated and bounced around.

In my defense, I was devasted and traumatized by the fact that my parents left me home alone at age ten and never returned. I'd spent days scared out of my mind until the police showed up, told me my parents had died in a car accident, and taken me to foster care.

For about four years, I was in and out of different homes—which often meant different schools—as the system tried to find my perfect fit. But it never worked out. I was too much work for the super crowded homes, too hard to handle for the quieter homes, and too damaged for the homes just wanting to look good in the eyes of the community. One home took me in and I was the only kid there, so I thought maybe it would be a permanent spot. Come to find out, they were only in it for the check and realized quickly that my attitude and nightmares weren't worth the measly amount of money. Kicked to the curb again.

A really nice couple took me in when I was thirteen, but when I got caught kissing a boy at school, they reported to the agency that they hadn't signed on for a gay child. What would their church say?

The night a social worker removed me from that home, I vowed to never again get my hopes up that a family would want me. My own parents hadn't been stellar, but at least I'd had a warm place to stay and food to eat. Before they died, I'd liked school—and been good at it—and had some friends. Their deaths took all of that from me.

And then I met Lilly.

"Hey, man. Gotcha some clothes from Rai. Let me show you the bathroom," Cruz broke into my thoughts. "Towels are in the closet. Soap and shampoo are in the shower, use any of them you want. Should be some new toothbrushes in the drawer, pick one." He gestured toward the bathroom before casting a glance at the backpack I still held—no way was I leaving it out of my sight. "Door locks. Take your time. I'll be back in the room you were just in. Dre is an EMT, he'll take a look at you and make sure you're not too banged up and then you can eat."

Nodding—because it was all my sore body and foggy head seemed capable of—I went into the bathroom and clicked the lock before leaning against the door and sighing in relief. The house was gorgeous and there were no alarms going off in my head like in the past. Earlier in the evening, I'd known the offer of twenty bucks was going to get me in trouble, but I'd ignored the warnings pinging in my mind.

The red alerts in my head weren't perfected way back when I'd met Lilly—no, she put those into place, albeit unintentionally, as she groomed me and sold me to the highest bidder.

When Lilly had just so happened to be working in the store where I stopped on my way home from school nearly every day during one of my longer—and final—foster placements, I'd taken no notice. She seemed like a nice lady who worked behind the counter. By the end of a month, thanks to her little gifts of free snacks and download codes and the coolest sneakers—which she said she'd bought her nephew and they didn't fit—I was convinced Lilly was the best thing ever. Why couldn't she be my foster mom?

And then Lilly offered me a place to stay. Said I

had to keep it secret, of course, because the agency wouldn't allow it. But she took me to her apartment a few towns over—looking back, I wondered why I never found it suspicious that she lived in such a nice place but drove nearly forty miles to work at a shitty corner store—and said I could have the spare room.

Pulling myself from my thoughts long enough to grab a towel and turn on the water, I brushed my teeth while the water warmed and then climbed in.

The hot water was fabulous and took me back to the first time I'd showered at Lilly's. She had a fancy double shower and I thought I'd died and gone to heaven.

Lilly promised me no more school woes and set me up with an online education program. Of all the things she put me through and took from me, I remained grateful to her for that program because I worked through it quickly and earned not only a GED, but also the equivalent of an associate's degree during the four years she trafficked me.

My gut roiled at the thought of how much those four years cost me, but I really was appreciative of the education.

Could have had an education and not been a sex slave.

Yeah, that would have been ideal.

I shampooed my hair and sighed as the warm water rained down.

Lilly had spent nearly a year showering me with gifts and making me feel like the luckiest kid around —found out later that she was able to spend that much time on me because she had several other kids she was already making money on.

And then the bottom fell out of my world.

Refusing to give much thought to the horrors she handed me over to, I soaped up and let water ease my aches and pains. I didn't know the ins and outs of all the working parts of her business, but suffice it to say that Lilly was a child predator who sold me to men, and a few women, who were willing to pay top dollar; there were likely a lot more people involved in the murky transactions, but Lilly was the only one, aside from buyers, I had any contact with.

By the time it all started, I was so indebted to her, so fearful of going back to foster care or being homeless, and so convinced that it was what I deserved, I had no choice but to do her bidding. When I balked, she threatened with the police. If I tried to refuse, she always sent me to the meanest buyers.

I learned quickly to just do as Lilly and the buyers asked and everything was a lot easier.

And then, when I was seventeen, everything changed.

As the water began to cool, I swallowed down the lump of fear threatening to overtake me and turned off the shower. I dried off and dressed, doing my best to style my hair with my fingers before picking up my ratty bag and heading back to Cruz's room. I wondered if Bev would let me wash my clothes and bag before I left.

"Feel better?" Cruz asked from the recliner in the corner. The room was tiny, but it held the bed, recliner, and a dresser easily, just not a lot of extra room.

"Yeah, thanks."

I jumped when someone knocked softly on the doorframe.

"Logan, this is Dre King, Bev's nephew," Cruz said. "Dre, this is Logan Miles."

"Hi, Logan. I'm an EMT. Cruz said you may have some injuries that need checked out?" Dre walked into the room with a box of medical supplies. His calm presence put me at ease and I couldn't help but return his soft smile. With his long, thick braids pulled back from his face, soulful brown eyes that matched his brown skin, and kind smile, I immediately liked Dre—the satin scarf, sharp black shirt, and fitted pants he wore didn't hurt either. "Can I take a look?"

I nodded and sat on the bed.

"I can leave," Cruz said as he stood from the recliner.

Immediately, I hated the idea. "Can you stay, please?" I asked in a whisper.

Cruz shot a look to Dre who nodded. Cruz sat back down.

"Thanks." I turned my attention to Dre. "I like your scarf. Actually, I like your whole outfit." It had been a long time since I'd been able to relax and just chat about something as mundane as clothing.

Dre smiled as he wrapped a blood pressure cuff around my arm. "Thanks. They're all Dre King originals."

I processed what he said and my eyes grew wide. "As in, you made them?"

"Dreamed up, designed, created, yep. I'm an EMT, but I'm also a fashion designer." Dre finished up with the blood pressure. "BP is normal."

"Like Hollywood?"

He shook his head. "No, I mean, I love all the red-carpet fashion and whatnot, but I want to make fabulous clothes for the everyday person. I'm not really a big city type person and I want to stay in Remington for a while, but I have big dreams of selling my designs and seeing my creations on regular people."

"That's awesome." I winced as Dre poked and prodded at some contusions.

"What do you do?" Dre asked.

I tensed. "Oh, um, nothing right now. I'm new to Remington. My plan to suck dick for a twenty didn't pan out so well tonight, so I'll be looking for another job hopefully sooner rather than later." My cheeks heated, but I figured it best to be honest.

"Stick around here and we'll get you set up," was all Dre said as he dabbed some ointment on an abrasion near my elbow.

"Oh, I can't stay," I said.

Dre glanced over at Cruz.

"I think Bev would like if you'd at least stay for a bit," Cruz said.

I frowned. "Why?"

Dre chuckled. "It's what my aunt does. She couldn't have children. After her husband died, she moved into this place with the thought of opening a bed and breakfast, but soon decided on a boarding house. She's a helper, a caregiver, and nothing makes her happier than providing a safe place for those who need it."

"So, everyone here is a loser like me?" I scoffed. "Seriously doubt that. Would I be the token sad case —the broken gay boy in need?" It was easier to be abrasive than to think about how badly I wanted to stay at Remington Place and how there was no way I could ever afford it. Sucking dick for twenty a pop barely kept me fed, let alone rich enough for a place like this.

Cruz cleared his throat and Dre laughed.

"Without going into a lot of details that aren't mine to tell," Dre began and fit a small bandage over a cut on my head, "you definitely aren't the only LGBTQ person here. Not the only person with a shitty past. Not the only person needing help. Guarantee it."

"You?" I asked.

"I'm queer, yeah. Can't decide on the label for me, but I'm not straight. Grew up in a super religious house and couldn't even admit it to myself until after high school. Traveled around trying to escape demons, tried college, nothing really fit. Decided on EMT and fashion—love helping people, but I use it as money to support my fashion—not that I make much. Came out to my parents recently, they told me I wasn't welcome at their home, so I ended up here with Aunt Bev."

I glanced toward Cruz, not allowing the question, but wondering.

He smirked. "Knew I was gay from the time I was a kid. Never acted on it or came out—church school and highly religious parents didn't lend to that type thing, ya know?" He shrugged. "Then I ended up in prison, parents died, haven't ever been somewhere longer than a month or so. Moving around so much doesn't exactly make for easy relationships. Always kinda felt like survival was more important than finding someone to fuck, ya know? Finally feel like I've found a home here in Remington."

"So, you've never had sex?" I couldn't help being shocked. Sex was such a conundrum for me. I wanted it and enjoyed it when it was my idea—or at least that's the way it seemed it would be in my head…I'd never had the chance for much sex outside of what Lilly sold me into—but loathed it when it wasn't within my control. I'd never been in a relationship, but I had wild fantasies about what being a boyfriend to a caring, loving guy would be like.

"Nah, I kept up appearances in high school. Didn't date a lot, but enough to never get questioned. Bad enough to be one of the only brown-skinned guys in the Catholic school, didn't need all the jocks getting any idea that I might be gay." Cruz glanced at Dre and I had a feeling maybe it was the first he'd shared that much with that particular housemate.

Dre nodded. "I think you're all good, no stitches needed and just some bruises that will heal."

"I've got food ready!" Bev hollered up the stairs.

"Let's go. We don't keep Bev waiting," Cruz said.

"Thank you, Dre," I said as he packed up his supplies. "Lucky me to get rescued by someone with an EMT roommate."

"Actually, he's got two medical roommates," Cruz said.

Dre rolled his eyes.

Cruz laughed. "Much to Dre's dismay, our newest roomie, who is Gabby's brother, is a paramedic and came to town to work on the same ambulance crew as Dre. Khi moved in right after I did."

Dre huffed. "He may have more schooling, but I'm the better roommate and first responder, don't forget it."

Cruz smirked. "You and Khi still putting all your efforts into avoiding each other?"

"Yep," Dre snapped. "Thank God we've been on different rigs, different shifts. When we're here, if we happen to be here at the same time, we stay out of each other's way."

"That's gotta be difficult when sharing a room," Cruz said.

"You and your roommate don't get along?" I asked.

"Understatement of the year," Cruz teased.

Dre cleared his throat. "We, um, knew each other

back in high school. Ran with different crowds, spent our time differently, completely contrasting personalities. No love lost between us."

I cocked my head. "That has to suck. Can you move rooms?"

Dre rolled his eyes. "No way, no how. Aunt Bev is convinced that Khi and I will eventually become friends if we're together enough."

I wrinkled my nose. "Bummer. Well, best of luck with that. Thanks again for patching me up."

"No worries, hope you're feeling better soon." Dre left the room.

"You okay?" Cruz asked.

"Yeah, I'm good. Just wanted to say thank you again. For stepping in and for bringing me here." I dipped my head and tried not to let my heart get fluttery about Cruz's dark hair, dark eyes, scruffy jaw, and broad shoulders. He was like protector incarnate. Despite my past, there was no doubt I found guys attractive—maybe it just happened a little less because so many men set off my red alert. Cruz set off warnings of a different sort, the kind that said he was just a nice guy helping me out and I needed to keep that in mind and not throw myself at him. But the thought of being warm in Cruz's arms, protected and safe, had me imagining all sorts of sexy scenarios.

Whatever. Look at you and look at him. He's clearly just a good Samaritan helping you out. He thinks of you as a kid. Even if you were closer in age, do you think a guy like Cruz would ever go for a guy like you?

"Not a problem. I really hope you'll stay for at least a while."

I bit my lip. "If I stay, will you be here?"

Cruz cocked his head. "I mean, I work next door at the auto shop and a few evenings and late nights a week at the Wishing Well, but other than that, I'm here pretty much all the time."

"And I'd stay in here with you?" I hitched my bag on my shoulder.

"I'll either take the floor or recliner or we'll get another bed in here." Cruz gestured.

"I'm going to sound pathetic, but for some reason, I feel safe with you. I can't afford to stay here, but if I were able to, I'd want to be in here with you." I glanced up and caught Cruz's eye.

"Let Bev talk about rent. But yeah, if you stay, I'll stay with you." Cruz's eyes shone bright. "But I promise, I'd never expect anything from you."

"I know. I don't know how I know, but I trust you completely. I know I'm safe with you." My cheeks heated.

Cruz reached out and ran a finger over the strap

of my bag. "You can leave your bag in here. I swear, no one will touch it."

I swallowed hard and nodded as I placed the bag in the far corner of the room just as my traitorous stomach grumbled.

"Come on, let's get you something to eat." Cruz chuckled and led me down the stairs.

THREE
CRUZ

My heart hurt as I watched Logan eat. He was too thin and I knew he'd likely been forced to skip meals when he couldn't get to a shelter.

"You're new to Remington?" Bev asked Logan as she handed me a sandwich.

I wasn't starving, but I knew Bev wanted me to eat so Logan would feel more comfortable. She was magical when it came to making people feel welcome in her home.

"Yes, ma'am," Logan said around a bite of food.

"I'd like to talk to you about staying here with us," Bev hedged. "Cruz, could you give us a moment?"

"Can he stay?" Logan asked, almost panicked.

Bev nodded. "Of course." She let him take a few more bites before continuing. "If you stay, you'll eventually find that several members of our little family have a bit of baggage they carry with them. We're all unique and we all have different needs. My offer of a place to stay isn't pity, I simply want to help when I can. I don't believe that anything happens randomly." She patted Logan's hand. "I think Cruz ended up at Remington Place so he'd be in the right place at the right time to help you. And I truly believe that you need this place as much as we need you. Why? Well, that remains to be seen, but I feel it in my heart that you belong here with us."

Logan's eyes were wide and he blinked rapidly against shiny tears. I had a feeling the evening and his past were catching up to him and he'd crash soon. "Ma'am, as much as I'd love a safe place to stay—truly haven't had that in a very long time—I have no job, not sure how I'll even get one, and no way to pay rent at this time. I'd like to stick around Remington for a while, the shelter here is really nice."

"How did you end up in Remington, if you don't mind me asking." Bev moved from his side and busied herself slicing pie and brewing tea.

Logan's eyes cut to mine.

"I can leave," I offered.

He shook his head. "No, may as well hear it as well."

Logan launched into a horrific story of losing his parents, moving from foster home to foster home, being trafficked by a woman named Lilly, and eventually escaping her at age seventeen.

I got the feeling he left out a few details— especially the part about how he got away from Lilly —and my gut clenched as he skimmed over the specifics of the nightmare he'd lived through. Suffice it to say, Logan had been forced into four years of cruel treatment and I wondered how he'd survived.

By the time he finished his story, all I wanted to do was wrap him in my arms and keep him safe from the world.

"Logan, I'm truly sorry for what you've been through. All the more reason for you to be safe and loved here." Bev cleared the dishes before handing Logan and me a slice of pie and gesturing toward the counter. "Grab your tea. Doctor it up if you'd like and meet me in the living room."

Logan dumped a few spoonfuls of sugar into his mug and I emptied a sweetener packet into mine before we followed Bev into the living room.

She sipped her tea before opening a notebook. "Rent for a room here is based on need. At this point in time, you have no means to pay rent, so we're going to bypass that for a moment."

Logan glanced toward me. I just nodded and

gestured to Bev with my chin. I recalled the evening she offered me a crazy low rent and how surreal it had been. I knew exactly what Logan was feeling.

"You need a job, or multiple jobs, to start bringing in some money. Do you have special skills?" Bev wrote on a page in her notebook.

Logan shrugged. "I have a GED and a general associate's degree. I like helping people and animals. I'm a good worker, but getting a job has always been hard because I don't have an ID or a permanent residence, plus I haven't stuck around any one place very long."

"Okay, we're going to talk to Jesse about getting you on at the Wishing Well to bus tables." Bev scribbled something. "I have a friend at both the animal shelter and the homeless shelter, I'll ask if they have an hour or two a day for extra help." She made another note. "What about the library?"

"I love libraries. Can't imagine a job at a library would be hard or unenjoyable," Logan answered.

"Do you think Cooper could give him some hours at the preschool?" I asked.

Bev pointed the pen at me. "That's a great idea."

"Preschool? I'd rather not work around kids— seeing kids in happy situations can sometimes trigger me and seeing kids in rough situations always triggers me, so it's best if I'm not immersed in kids

—but I can do any kind of before or after-hours work."

"Cooper and Jesse have a daughter, Hadley, who spends a lot of time here." Bev glanced up with concern in her eyes. "Will that be a problem?"

Logan shook his head. "Probably not. If it is, I'll take a break."

"Just as a side note," I began, "Hadley hasn't had the easiest life, but she's kinda getting a happy ending in a way."

Logan cocked a brow.

"Her mom and grandma were killed in a car wreck when she was an infant." My heart clenched when Logan's eyes clouded and I knew he was thinking of losing his own parents in the same way. "Jesse is biologically her grandfather, but he's been raising her since then. To look at them, Cooper and Jesse should have no business together—there's a twenty-five-year age gap and they have very different personalities—but I honestly don't know if I've ever seen two people more in love." I cocked my head. "Maybe Spencer and Rai, but my point is that you and Hadley may have a bit in common. She's thriving ever since moving to Remington and she adores having Jesse and Cooper as her dads."

"Yeah, I don't see how a kid like Hadley would be much of a trigger for me." Logan shrugged. "It's not like I don't want kids to be safe, happy, and loved, I just sometimes get depressed at all I lost. The biggest triggers are when I see or suspect kids are in a bad situation and I get anxious. I want to help, but I don't know how, and I worry that maybe I'm projecting my past onto them and reading the situation wrong. That's usually when I go into a tailspin. I think being around Hadley will be fine." He smiled softly. "I love that she's getting a happy ending."

"Okay, that sounds good. But you feel free to take a break or speak up if you're feeling any anxiety." She tapped her pen. "We'll get some jobs lined up." Bev clucked her tongue as she wrote. "But we need to get you an ID and that could be tough depending on required documents."

"I have my birth certificate and my social security card," Logan offered.

Bev's eyes widened. "Oh, well, those two things will be a game changer for sure. How do you have those items?"

He smirked. "I stole them from the agency before I went to live with Lilly. I keep them hidden in a book in my backpack. I've never stayed anywhere long enough to go to the trouble of getting a state ID."

"Well, we'll still need a couple things. Let's get

you a library card. I think you need a photo ID for that, but I can maybe sign as a parent? We'll see. What about a bank account?"

Logan bristled. "Don't really want to give my money to a bank."

"I get that," I interjected. "But if you get a bank account, your money is a lot safer in the bank than in your backpack. Plus, you'll be able to use mail from the bank as proof of residency for the state ID." I knew this because Bev had recently helped me do the same. "And you can get a safe deposit box to keep your valuables in."

"You've done all this?" Logan asked.

I nodded. "Yep. It's kinda a pain, but it's better in the long run."

He took a deep breath. "Okay, let's do all of it." Scowling, he glanced at Bev. "But once I have a job, what's rent going to be?"

I knew Bev didn't like to talk about the various rents she charged around her boarders, so I took everyone's mugs. "I'll be right back. Can I get anyone anything?" Knowing Bev would use the time to give Logan a rent amount that was totally doable, I took a moment to rinse the mugs before returning to the living room.

Logan's face held shock and he kept blinking as if trying to come out of a dream.

"Okay," Bev barreled on, "we'll get started on the ID, bank account, and library card tomorrow. I'm going to draw up that rent contract, get it notarized, and mail it to you here at Remington Place as another proof of residency. We'll put out some feelers for jobs, too." Bev closed her notebook. "Now, you'll need to meet everyone, but for now, you need sleep. You and Cruz talk about your arrangements. Squeeze a twin bed in? Both of you take twins? Share the queen? Floor? Recliner? It's up to the two of you." Bev stood.

I mentally made the sign of the cross. I did not need to share a bed with Logan. Not that I didn't want to, but being in the same bed would make things very hard—both literally and figuratively. Surely, he wouldn't be comfortable sharing a bed with a man he'd just met. I'd offer to take the floor or recliner for that night and we'd look into moving the twin in the next day.

"We have family dinner every Thursday with Cooper, Jesse, and Hadley. I fix an evening meal every day for anyone who's here. Groceries I buy are for everyone; if you want something extra, ask or buy it yourself. Don't bring drama into my house and show everyone respect. Once you start paying rent, it's due on the first or last and if you get in a bind, you talk to me. Communication is key. A lot of

problems can be avoided or fixed just by talking."
She pulled Logan into a hug. "We're family here and
glad to have you with us."

Tears streamed down Logan's face by that point
and I couldn't help putting an arm around him as
Bev made her way from the living room.

Not expecting it, I tensed when Logan turned in
my arms and buried his face against my chest. With
very little thought, I wrapped my arms around his
slim body and held him close. He was about two
inches shorter than my five-foot-ten-inches, and I
outweighed him by a good fifty pounds. But he fit
against me perfectly. I had to take a few deep breaths
to remind myself that he was a new roommate in
need, not a potential hookup.

As if you're any kind of expert on potential
hookups. You've had very few interactions with men
and this is not the time to start thinking about the
possibility.

I knew my head was right. Aside from the age
difference and his hellish past, there were several
reasons I had no business thinking of Logan as
anything but a new friend. I wanted to be sure he
was safe and cared for, had a chance to get on his
feet, and could finally relax and find his home. There
was nothing else I needed to think about Logan. No
matter how good he felt pressed against me, how

soft he felt in my arms, how good he smelled, or how curious and hungry his blue eyes were when he finally pulled back to look at me from under a floppy fringe of light brown hair.

"Come on, let's get to bed. You look exhausted." I maneuvered Logan toward the stairs and followed him up.

"Oh, hey," Rai said when we met him at the top. "Hi, I'm Raiden Ono."

Spencer stuck his head out of their room and joined us. "I'm Spencer Nelson."

Logan shook hands. "I'm Logan Miles."

"You going to stay with us?" Rai asked.

"I'm thinking about it." Logan shuffled and looked at the floor.

"You totally should." Rai put his arm around Spencer's waist. "My parents kicked me out when I came out. Spent years couch surfing, sleeping on floors, and living in my car from time-to-time."

Spencer leaned over and kissed Rai's head.

"Spencer invited me over to meet Bev and my life changed. This is seriously the best place I've ever lived."

"And it's only partly because he fell in love with me," Spencer teased.

It was funny to watch the two of them together. They were very different, and Spencer was pretty stoic and gruff by himself, but when Rai was by his side, he came to life. I'd moved in right as Spencer and Rai were figuring out their relationship, but I'd heard stories that it was a bit of a mess for a while. Supposedly, though, Cooper and Jesse had been in a very similar situation before they finally worked it out.

No wonder Bev had made me promise no drama.

The thought gave me pause. No drama. Pretty sure getting involved with a guy fifteen years my junior when he was only supposed to be sharing my room would be considered drama. Yet another reason to lock down any attraction I may have been feeling toward Logan. Immediately.

"Thanks. It's really nice here. I'd like to stay." Logan yawned. "Sorry, I'm about to fall over."

"No worries, get some rest. Hopefully you'll stick around. See ya later." Rai gave a little wave as he pulled Spencer back into their bedroom.

When we entered our room, I noticed Logan's eyes quickly went to the corner to check on his bag. His fists clenched and I figured he was dying to make sure everything was where it was supposed to be.

"Open it up," I gestured toward his bag, "I promise everything is safe."

Logan grabbed his bag and took it with him to sit on the bed. He emptied the contents and my heart stuttered to think the kid's whole life fit in a damn dirty backpack.

"Do you think Bev would be okay with me washing the bag and some dirty clothes?" Logan's hand closed on a plastic bag that I guessed were dirty clothes.

"Definitely. We can do laundry in the morning, no problem."

Logan rifled through the items. Picking up a worn hardback, he opened it and peeled back a layer of the back cover to reveal a flat plastic bag. "My birth certificate and social security card."

As if needing the moment, Logan began to show me each item with a brief description. "I never have much money, but I keep it in this lock box. Keep the key in my shoe most of the time." His fingers trailed over the edge of the small metal box. "Socks, underwear, washcloths. Always did my best to stay clean. Showered and washed up whenever possible. Used the laundromat when I'd get enough money to run a load." He chuckled dryly when he picked up a phone and charger. "No minutes, not sure why I even kept it. Picked it up when I first left Lilly, but couldn't afford to keep the minutes on it as time went by."

I remembered what it was like to have my possessions taken from me, but for some reason, watching Logan take stock of such meager belongings hurt my heart more than anything I'd been through in prison. "What about that one?" I pointed toward a thread-bare stuffed rabbit.

Logan sniffed. "That's Bunny. I've had him since I was a baby. He was a gift from my only living relative at the time, my grandma. She died when I was three I think. Not having any family is why I ended up in foster care. Although, to hear Mom and Dad talk about their childhoods, I'm guessing living with relatives wouldn't have been much better." He picked up the stuffed animal and rubbed his nose against Bunny's head while caressing one of the toy's ears. "I used to rub his ears to fall asleep. I know it's beyond pathetic for a grown man to have a stuffed animal, but he's like my only connection to my parents." Logan glanced up at me with shiny eyes. "Don't get me wrong. My parents weren't perfect, but losing them sent me into a hellish seven-year nightmare that got worse with every passing moment. Maybe they would have eventually kicked me out if they'd found out I was gay, I really don't know—I was only ten and remember having some idea that I maybe liked boys, but it wasn't something I'd given a lot of thought to before they died. Guess I'll never know for sure, but I have a feeling Mom would have maybe been okay and Dad would have been completely against it." He shrugged. "Either way, no kid should have to be bounced from place to place hoping and praying for someone, anyone, to take him in. And then to be sold and used for sex..." Logan shivered and his eyes took on a faraway look for several moments before he pulled himself from his thoughts and turned to me. "Can I be honest about something?"

"Of course, always." I sat on the bed.

"Part of me is so relieved to be here. I want so badly for this to be real and for it to work. I usually have a pretty good sense about people and I want to trust that my gut is right about you and Bev, hell, I didn't even feel anxiety with Dre or Rai or Spencer."

"But?"

Logan tucked Bunny against his chest and pulled his knees up tight. "I didn't realize Lilly was a dangerous, terrible person until it was too late. She made me feel wanted and gave me all this great stuff." He kept his face buried against his knees. "What if I'm just falling for it again? What if I'm so desperate for food, a warm bed, and love that I'm ignoring warning signs and I'll be stuck in the nightmare all over again?"

I was quiet for a moment as I thought through his words. Damn, I could totally see his point.

"I know, I sound like a crazy ungrateful psycho," Logan mumbled.

"No, I get it. I'm not a professional, so I don't have any answers for you, but I get what you're saying." I shifted on the bed and pulled my knee under me. "I've only been here a few months, but I can assure you I've seen nothing suspicious, illegal, dangerous, or immoral going on—and I saw a lot in my past thanks to friends tied up in gangs and then my time in prison." I gritted my teeth, wishing I could help Logan feel safe. "Cooper, Dalton, Gabby, and Spencer have been here since the beginning. Cooper is a licensed preschool teacher who opened his own preschool. That takes background checks, so I'm sure he's on the up-and-up. Dalton and Gabby have jobs in some big office and I know they work with money so I'm sure they have to be checked from time-to-time. I think Jesse had social services checking in on him for a while after his wife and daughter were killed and he had sole custody of Hadley. Dre and Khi are first responders, so I'd think they'd been trustworthy." I sighed. "Look, I know every detail I'm giving has a counterargument. I don't know that there's a solid answer for how I know this place is nothing like Lilly's. I understand your hesitation. Maybe you take it day-by-day? At the first indication of warning flags, you can leave."

Logan shuddered, breathing deeply as he sniffed and lifted his head. "Yeah, that may be my best bet. I just keep getting these flashbacks to Lilly. I was so grateful and relieved when she took me in and then it all turned to shit. I just don't want to make the same mistake again. It's so damn hard to trust people."

"I get that. You've been through things that no one should ever have to experience. I'm surprised you're even comfortable being around men at all."

Logan shrugged. "It's not just men. Lilly would sometimes sell me to women. But it was mostly men." He swallowed and got that faraway look in his eyes again. "She almost always watched, sick fucker," Logan bit out. "She said it was to make sure I was safe, but she sure as hell never did anything about it when the buyers would get rough." He shivered again. "She always told me I was lucky she liked me and she didn't sell me to women very often. Said I was one of her favorites so she always tried to make sure I got sold to men since she knew I was gay." He closed his eyes and sighed. "When she was grooming me, making me feel loved and wanted and valued, I made the mistake of telling her I was gay. Told her all about the boys I had crushes on. She told me she loved me and accepted me no matter what. Really wished I'd never told her; she didn't deserve to know the real me." He huffed. "It's kinda amazing to me that I even still find men attractive after all that was done to me." He glanced up at me. "Believe me, a lot of men—and some women—give me the creeps and I can't get away from them fast enough." He cocked his head. "But no one here has given me that vibe and I feel amazingly calm around you. To be honest, it's kinda freakin' me out a bit. Like, is my safety system screwed up? Am I no longer able to judge if a person is good or bad?" Logan licked his lips. "Or have I just miraculously landed in a safe-zone with a bunch of really good people?"

I smiled. "I'd like to think it's the latter, but I can see how it would be hard to trust."

"From the moment the police came to my house and told me my parents were dead, I've never once had anything good or miraculous happen to me. Even things that seemed good would turn bad." He rested his forehead against his knees. "So, it's definitely hard to think that I've found a safe home with these great people." He looked up again. "The only part I'm not questioning is you. Which sounds ridiculous, I know. But from the moment you stepped into that alley, I knew I could trust you."

"So, why'd you think I wanted you to suck me off for a place to stay?"

Logan scoffed. "Abrasive and negative is my go-to. Sex acts are a form of currency in my life. I didn't really think you were asking for sex in exchange for a place to stay, but it was easier to go there than try to believe someone was really offering to help." He covered his eyes with his hand. "I don't know if that makes any sense. My head is so fucked up."

"Some of the housemates go to a psychiatrist named Alicia. She could maybe help," I offered.

"I doubt it. Plus, I don't have insurance and probably can't afford her."

"You don't have insurance?" I scowled.

"Hello? No address, no job, no ID—voila, no insurance." Logan rolled his eyes. "That's why I avoid hospitals. They say they'll treat anyone despite their ability to pay, but no ID card and no insurance and no mailing address always brings in the social workers and it's a mess, so I just don't go." Logan carefully packed everything back into his bag.

"I think Bev can help with the insurance as well; she has a lot of contacts and resources. And I think Alicia offers a sliding scale for payment." I stood from the bed. "Maybe worth checking out."

Logan gave a little nod and shrugged. "We'll see."

Accepting it as a tiny win, I dropped the subject. "You need the bathroom before bed?"

He took advantage of my offer and came back to the room smelling of soap and toothpaste so I

figured he'd washed his face and brushed his teeth.
My heart squeezed as I realized that, even in prison,
I had access to things Logan had been forced to go
without just to escape the nightmares of his past.

Logan climbed into bed. "I don't mind to share a
bed, at all. I'd rather you not be on the floor or in
that chair."

"It's no big deal," I answered much too quickly.

"I mean, at your age, sleeping on the floor or in a
recliner can't be good for your back," Logan teased
with bright eyes and his bottom lip caught between
his teeth.

Gaping, not sure whether to laugh or be offended
at his mouthy little comment, I narrowed my eyes.
Pointing my finger, I decided to join his game.
"Children should be seen and not heard. You need to
respect your elders, young man."

Logan giggled and it was the most amazing sound
I'd ever heard. As if ten years of terror lifted from
him, his gorgeous face lit up like life had been
breathed into him. "I'm guessing you won't be able
to see or hear me soon. Vision and hearing are
usually the first to go as you age. Hearing aids and
bifocals are probably happening soon."

"You're a mouthy little shit, you know that?" I
left the room and came back with a blanket. "Toss
me that pillow."

Logan grinned as he threw a pillow toward me. "All joking aside, I'd feel better if you just slept in the bed."

"I'll be fine in the chair." Despite the words, I wanted nothing more than to climb into bed and hold Logan close. What kind of fucked up situation had I found myself in?

He stared at me for a moment before crawling under the covers and turning off the bedside lamp. "Thank you for today."

"No worries. Anyone would have done the same."

"No, they wouldn't. Believe me, I know." He was quiet for a moment. "And I'm glad it was you. You're something special."

Letting the warmth of his words wash over me, I settled into the recliner with a smile. It had been a long time since anyone had made me feel special. It was kinda nice.

FOUR
LOGAN

THE NIGHTMARES WERE USUALLY ALL the same. Or at least a mixed bag of the same scenes over and over.

Flashes of the buyers using me, recollections of my screams and the threats of more if I didn't just do as asked, hours left alone to clean up and relax before being put back in the lineup for the whole horrific ordeal to begin again.

Sometimes, the bad dreams would change things up and throw in my last few months with Lilly. The new kid. Fuck, he was so young, barely thirteen. Same as I had been, but it was hard to remember being that innocent. And knowing what he faced had thrown me into a tailspin of anxiety and nausea.

My nightly visions were filled with scenes of Lilly grooming Rusty, telling me all that she hoped to do with him, all the money he'd bring in, which buyers were already frothing at the mouth to get hold of him. By the time Lilly brought Rusty around, she'd already gotten her claws into him and he couldn't see the threat—just like me way back then—and by the time he'd realize what a monster she was, it would be too late. We'd both be stuck.

And then the dreams would skip ahead.

Lilly bleeding on the floor.

Me screaming at Rusty to follow me as I grabbed my backpack and stuffed as much in it as possible.

Shoving him toward the agency door before I disappeared and began my three-year run from shelter to shelter. I was seventeen at the time. Way too old to go back into foster care and scared to death that Lilly would find me again if I did. Rusty was younger and maybe had a chance. He couldn't go with me so I had to leave him at the agency. Leaving him at Lilly's or out on his own would have been a death sentence for the kid.

I came awake slowly, the remnants of that night's bad dream just barely out of reach as I tried to wrap my head around what had happened and where I was.

The nightmares where I'd see Lilly bleeding on the floor, while not as painful as recalling the pain and horror I experienced at the hand of the buyers, always left me unsettled. I couldn't remember what led up to Lilly busting her head on the floor. Didn't remember how she busted her head or what I did after finding her that way. My subconscious mind always moved from Lilly's plans for Rusty to finding her on the ground to leaving Rusty at the agency and it drove me insane to know I was missing pieces of my memories.

Sitting up, glancing around the room and slowly remembering I was at Remington Place, I took a deep breath. Nightmares were normal for me. Waking up and realizing I was warm and safe was completely new.

I caught sight of Cruz in the recliner. His long legs hung over the foot rest and his arms stretched over his head. In the dim light from the window, I took in the dark hair on his chest, the slightly muscled abdomen, and the trail of hair beneath his naval leading under his boxers. The blanket Cruz had grabbed from the hall closet was draped over his thighs, but not his muscular calves. He wasn't a super built man, but he had a gorgeous body and I found myself smiling at the thought of all I wanted to do to him.

Maybe I did need to see a therapist because I was pretty damn confident that I was truly screwed up. With all I'd been through, the violence and violations, how could I still find someone attractive and want physical intimacy with him?

I knew I had two very separate compartments in my head—when I was younger, I didn't realize I'd begun to differentiate, but as I got older, it was easy to see my head was doing its best to keep me sane and away from the bad shit.

All of the horrific parts of my past—the people, the acts, the pain—those were all packed tightly away and I only allowed myself brief glimpses into that compartment, even though the memories came out in nightmares and during my lowest times whether I wanted them to or not.

The other compartment, almost like a desk drawer I could open and rifle through at will, contained what I considered normal thoughts and fantasies about everything from clothing and shoes I found appealing to future hopes and dreams I held for myself to dating and, yes, even sex.

The sex in this compartment was all under my control. I dreamed of it, I wanted it, I asked for it, I initiated it. Nothing was ever forced or harsh or degrading. This little drawer contained everything good about relationships and intimacy that I hoped to one day experience.

My past was locked in the first compartment.

I said a little prayer that my future was in the second.

And I wanted Cruz in that future.

You're a damn idiot if you think a guy fifteen years older than you would want to get mixed up with your level of shit show. You think Cruz wants to deal with all of your baggage? What would he possibly find attractive about your slim build and used body? Plus, you just met the guy!

Lifting my chin in defiance of my thoughts, I stared at Cruz as he slept. He had stepped in and helped me. He had invited me to his home. He'd promised to stay with me. He'd hugged me close and told me I was wanted.

Was it possible that I had a bit of hero worship going on? Definitely. But with all I'd been through, that wasn't really surprising.

But what I felt for Cruz was more than just idolizing my rescuer.

Or at least I wanted it to be.

Was it crazy to feel this way about a man I'd met mere hours before? Yeah, I could admit that. But there was something about Cruz that spoke to my heart and told me he was safe and special.

Cruz was the first guy I'd trusted enough to want anything more with. More often than not, I was creeped out or scared to death of men. And if I wasn't, like with Dalton, Dre, Spencer, and Rai, I felt comfortable with them platonically, but never sexually.

Cruz was different.

I knew I'd have to convince him and I knew it would have to move slowly.

But I needed and wanted Cruz in my life, both as a friend and as more.

And if he says no?

I frowned. I'd never push a person into something they weren't okay with. If Cruz wanted to keep things as just friends, I'd respect that.

I'd hate it.

But I'd respect it.

"Cruz," I whispered across the room. "Cruz?"

He stirred in his chair and sat up with a start. "Logan? What's wrong? You okay?"

"Nightmares. Can you please sleep with me?" I bit my lip and waited. I wasn't acting, wasn't trying to manipulate. I truly just wanted Cruz beside me.

He sighed. "Logan, I really don't know if that's a good idea."

"Please? I'm just freaked out and lonely."

He closed his eyes and pinched the bridge of his nose before tossing the blanket to the floor and standing from the chair.

I scrambled to the wall side of the bed and made room for Cruz to climb in.

"We need to talk," Cruz mumbled.

"In the morning. Promise." I cuddled against Cruz's chest and got comfy. "We do need to talk, I agree. Bev's right, communication is key. But for now, can we just sleep?"

Cruz grunted and tentatively wrapped an arm around me before a breath whooshed from him. "First thing in the morning. We need some guidelines or something." His words sounded pained, but he pulled the blanket up over us and buried his face in my hair.

For the first time since my parents died, I slept comfortably.

COMING AWAKE with Cruz's warmth at my back, I smiled softly. I knew he wanted to talk, and it was probably for the best, but I just wanted to savor the safe, protected feeling for a few moments longer.

Cruz awoke and tension filled his body. He didn't exactly push me away, but he untangled our arms and legs and moved to the edge of the bed. Throwing his pillow over his hips, Cruz groaned.

I rolled over to face him and frowned when he

ran a hand over his face. "I'm sorry if last night made you uncomfortable."

He shook his head. "No, it wasn't you. The whole situation is just weird."

"Weird how?" I propped my head on my hand.

"Finding you in the alley, bringing you home, setting you up here." Cruz shrugged one shoulder. "I've only been getting back on my feet for a short time, it doesn't really feel like I should be in this role as helper, but it seemed natural to step in and help you."

"I really appreciate everything you did for me." I studied him for a moment. "What else seems weird? I get the feeling that's not all."

Cruz buried his face in the crook of his arm. "Okay, real talk?"

"Seems like we've both had some very real shit in our lives, keeping it real between us is probably for the best."

"I'm gay, but I've not really done a lot with guys. Haven't done anything with girls since high school, but that was all just for show. I think I already mentioned that I kept my sexuality hidden in high school. Then, when I ended up in prison, it didn't exactly feel like the safest place to be coming out. I've been moving from place to place for eight years and that doesn't leave a lot of time for relationships or even finding hookups. Survival mode doesn't leave a person feeling very sexy…"

"Don't I know it," I whispered.

Cruz uncovered his face to reveal a scowl and reached for my hand. "Yeah, you probably get it more than anyone would. So, kisses, blow jobs, a couple quick fucks in a gas station bathroom is my resume of gay sex. Not stellar."

"In the hope of keeping it real—while not completely freaking you out—my resume of gay sex is blank." When Cruz looked confused, I continued. "Yeah, I've had a lot done to me, forced on me. But none of it has been welcome or wanted. I got caught kissing a boy at school right before I met Lilly. That's the only thing I've ever done that was my idea. So, even though you're probably grossed out by all the things I was forced to do, I'm a virgin when it comes to safe, consensual sex. And even more so with intimacy of any kind. I think that's why having you in bed to cuddle was such a comfort. It was something I longed for—I wanted and needed your warmth and protection."

Cruz moved from holding my hand to cupping my chin and making my eyes meet his. "Hey, I may be pissed and sick to my stomach at all that was done to you—to the point where I'd love to gather a group and hunt down each and every one of those fuckers—but that has nothing to do with how I see you. You are not at fault. Your body is not gross or used, don't you ever think that. You are beautiful and good inside and out."

Tears filled my eyes as Cruz's words washed over me. "Thanks. No one has ever said that to me."

Cruz wiped a tear from my cheek. "With all that being said…"

"Uh-oh, here it comes." I huffed and rolled my eyes. "Let me guess. This is where you claim to be much too old for me and you take the high road by letting me work through my demons without clouding my young, naïve mind with conflicting feelings of sex versus friendship."

Cruz blinked rapidly. "Well…" he frowned, "yeah. I'm fifteen years older than you. We've both been through some shit, but I've had a longer time to heal and get my shit together. You're still…"

"Suffering? Yeah, Cruz, I'll likely always suffer from the horrors I lived through. But I don't want to live my entire life waiting and wanting just because of shit in my past that was out of my control." I sat up and crossed my legs. "I like you and that's a completely new situation for me. Yeah, I've found other guys attractive ever since escaping Lilly, but it's more with you."

Cruz smiled softly. "I like you, too."

"And that bothers you?"

He pursed his lips before speaking. "It bothers me for a few reasons. One, you're young. Two, you've got a lot of healing to do. Three, maybe this is just some sort of hero complex where I think I have to save you, save the day, be the big bad protector."

"I get that." I really did; I was having some of the same thoughts. "Honestly, though, your age means nothing to me. Maybe it's because of my past— buyers were every age you could imagine—but nothing about you being thirty-five bothers me. Yes, I have healing to do—so do you if I'm not mistaken —but having a support system of friends and family seems like the best way to heal." I held my hand out and thrilled when he took it and held it tight in his own. "I'm grateful for you rescuing me and I can see where maybe you're dealing with a hero complex, but maybe I'm dealing with hero worship."

"We're a pair, huh?" Cruz laughed with no humor.

"I'm just saying, we'll likely need to work through a lot of things. Maybe I'll see about that Alicia lady and doing some therapy. But us being close doesn't seem like a bad thing." I brushed my thumb over the back of Cruz's hand.

"Close?"

I smiled. "Don't worry, I'm not ready for anything

more than friends right now. So, let's lay those ground rules, huh?"

Cruz took a deep breath and nodded. "Okay, tell me what you need."

"And you tell me your limits, this is a two-way street." A flutter of hope filled my chest. Had anyone ever asked me what I needed?

He nodded. "I've gotta be honest and say this all seems beyond surreal."

"But you're not uncomfortable or feeling pushed into anything?"

Cruz shook his head.

"Okay, so first things first, can we just keep the big bed and share it? I slept better last night than I have in about ten years." I pictured Cruz and I wrapped in a cocoon of cozy warmth night after night, but then something else struck me like a lead balloon. "Oh, um, if you want to have someone else in your bed, I can take the couch downstairs on those nights."

Cruz's brow furrowed and then he chuckled. "Logan, I haven't had a man in my bed my entire life, pretty sure starting with and sticking to just one will be plenty for me."

My heart danced. "Okay, well, we can revisit the topic as needed." Over my dead body would I easily give up Cruz to another man, but that wasn't an issue for the time being. "I'll sleep next to the wall for two reasons. One, because it makes me feel safer. Two, because men your age have to get up to pee a lot so being on the edge will make it easier for you."

Cruz narrowed his eyes. "For someone who claims my age doesn't bother them, you sure have all sorts of jokes. Mouthy little shit is what you are," he teased.

I smiled and batted my lashes. "I am not against intimate moments, but I'm not ready for them yet. Are you okay with that?"

Cruz cleared his throat. "Um, yeah. Intimate how?"

"Kissing and touching? I want those things, but I need to be the one to initiate. If we get to that point, and you're not okay with it, just say the word." I shifted back to stretch out on my side.

"So, we're friends but we cuddle, sleep together, and maybe at some point kiss and touch?"

"Yes? Is that okay?" I bit my lip.

Cruz huffed and smirked. "Different type of friendship than I've ever had, but if it's what you need, I can handle it."

"I don't want you doing it just because it's what you think I need. I want you to be comfortable with it." I frowned.

He reached for my hand again. "It's fine. After I

got over the shock of last night, I slept better with you in my bed than I have in a long time." He cleared his throat. "What about moving past kissing and touching? I'd never force that, you'd have to be in total control of the when and where. But is it something you think you'd want?"

I shivered. "In my fantasies, yes. In reality? I don't know." My bottom lip curled down as a thought hit me. "Maybe this isn't fair to you." Dropping my head, I buried my face in the pillow. "I'm sorry, I can't believe I'm asking you to do this."

"Hey," Cruz whispered as he lifted my face to look at him, "it's okay. I wasn't looking to date or hookup or anything. I find you so damn attractive I have to check my chin from time to time to make sure I'm not drooling. I promise having you in bed and maybe working our way toward more isn't going to be a problem for me." He winked. "Maybe a lot of cold showers and jerking off, but that's pretty much par for the course so no worries."

"Thanks," I whispered. "I feel the same about you. Honestly, I could strip you down and ride you right here and now with no qualms."

Cruz's eyes went wide and he swallowed thickly.

"But it wouldn't be me. It would be the me of the past, the one who shuts down and just lets the sex happen in hopes of a warm meal or money or surviving, and I don't want that with you." I breathed through the rapid beating of my heart. "If and when we have sex, I want it to be right. I want it to be Logan and Cruz and none of my demons." I sniffed and blinked away tears. "I know it can happen because my demons go away when I'm with you—and, dear God, how crazy does that sound when I've known you less than a day, but it's the truth—so I know when we move into something more it will be the real Logan. I just need time to work up to that."

"You've got all the time you need." Cruz cupped my cheek. "And if you never get to that part, you'll always have me as a friend. We may have an unconventional relationship, and it does seem crazy that we're even having this conversation less than twenty-four hours from meeting, but if it works for us then screw anyone who may question it."

"You'll tell me if you ever need out? Need to move on and date someone else?"

Cruz nodded. "I will. And you'll do the same?"

I smiled. "Sure." Not likely to happen, but I'd placate him.

"Then I guess we're friends who cuddle and sleep together for now?" Cruz asked.

"And support each other, hang out, and learn to heal?"

"Definitely." Cruz brushed a thumb over my cheek. "Gotta say, this is the weirdest start to a friendship I've ever had."

I laughed. "Me, too. But that's okay, I kinda love it."

"We better get downstairs for breakfast. Bev doesn't like when she cooks and no one is there to eat it." Cruz rolled from the bed and pulled on a pair of lounge pants. "We'll see what she thinks about job hunting and getting an ID today."

I scrambled from bed and pulled on the clothes I'd borrowed from Rai. "Knowing breakfast is just down there, waiting on me is so surreal. Can you show me the washing machine today?"

"Yep, and we should go grab you some new clothes." Cruz yanked a shirt over his head.

"I don't have a lot of money." I worried my bottom lip. "Maybe I can just wear my old stuff until I get a job?"

"How about I loan you some money and you can pay me back? Friends do that, right?" Cruz opened the bedroom door and gave me a wink.

Somehow, I knew that my friendship with Cruz was going to change my life forever. And for the first time in over a decade, a real sense of hope and happiness bloomed in my chest.

FIVE
CRUZ

I was living in the Twilight Zone. That was the only way to explain the situation with Logan and me. On one hand, I wanted to write the whole thing off as Logan being way too young with a terrible past glomming onto me with some sort of infatuation.

But doing that wouldn't be quite fair.

Because I'd somehow formed this strange attachment to him from the moment I found him on the ground out back of the Wishing Well. He was cute as fuck, mouthy, and had a lot of shit to work through. But I found myself drawn to him like nothing I'd ever experienced before.

So, I finished up my Twilight Zone breakfast, knowing Bev and pretty much the whole gang were watching me and Logan, and decided to just go with the flow of the day. Maybe I'd talk to Jesse or Dre later. Maybe even Khi? But that man hadn't let his guard down since the moment he moved in and the tension between him and Dre was crazy thick. Perhaps Khi wasn't my best bet for conversation right then.

"I'm going to get Logan set up with the washing machine and take him to get some clothes," I told Bev as we sipped our coffee. "What are the plans for jobs and an ID card?"

Bev smiled. "Well, I've been talking to people already this morning. Logan, once you get your ID card, you'll have some interviews at the Wishing Well, the library, and the animal shelter. Cooper doesn't want an interview, just wants you to let him know when you can start; he's going to have you refilling paint and glue pots, washing paint brushes, and organizing supplies a few days a week after hours."

Logan's eyes grew wide and a smile filled his precious face. "That sounds great. So do the other places. I can't wait; I want to feel needed and productive. Where do I need to start for getting an ID card?"

"We'll go to the BMV once you get the library card, bank account, and mail in your name from our rent contract." Bev washed her coffee cup and left it to dry. "Now, something we didn't discuss—and it won't affect what you need to get the ID—but are you wanting to get a driver's license? If so, we need to prepare for the driving and written tests assuming you've never had those before."

A look of terror passed over Logan's face. "I don't want to drive. Maybe ever." He took a deep breath and glanced around the table. I knew he'd see only support in the faces of our housemates, but my heart still hurt for the kid. "I guess being left alone and then finding out a car wreck killed your parents changes how you look at one of the big milestones of a kid's life. Driving scares me. I don't mind being in a vehicle, but the act of actually driving gives me a lot of anxiety."

"Okay, ID only then. We can talk about a driver's license if you ever change your mind." Bev gestured toward the utility room. "Cruz, get him set up with laundry and new clothes. We'll do library and bank after."

I took a deep breath. "We probably should check in at the police station about last night." I cast a glance toward Logan and hated the way his face fell.

"Can't we just ignore it? Pretend it didn't happen?"

Shrugging, I placed a hand on his shoulder. "Let's just go and see what they know. I'll tell them my part, you tell them yours. If they didn't catch the assholes you won't even have to worry about pressing charges or not."

"And if they did?" Logan's words were barely a whisper.

"Then it's totally your call and we'll support you no matter what," Bev interjected and I nodded with a squeeze to Logan's shoulder.

A few hours later, Logan had a freshly washed backpack, new clothes, and a stack of laundered old items.

"Go ahead and put things in your drawers." I pointed to the drawers I'd cleared for him. "If you need more room, we can share."

"Nah, I think I'll be fine with these plus the hangers in the closet. I'm not going to need to dress up for any of the jobs, so the jeans and shirts we got will be more than enough." He put four shirts and a zip-up jacket on hangers. "Thank you again for the clothes, I promise I'll pay you back."

"It's not a problem. You needed some clothes for your job interviews and starting work. You're set up now." I took a pair of new jeans and folded them before placing them in the drawer. "I know you'll pay me back. It's not like I don't know where you live."

He smiled, but I knew he was thinking about something.

"You okay?"

Logan nodded. "I can't decide if I'm glad they didn't catch the guys from the alley or not." With a shrug he put the rest of his clothes in the closet. "Those two assholes didn't hurt me any more than so many others in my past; making them pay wouldn't make the shit show I lived through go away."

I waited and let him process his thoughts.

He bit his lip and sighed. "Like, I didn't want the inconvenience of pressing charges, but I guess I kinda wish they'd been caught. Not a lot would have probably happened, but I guess it would have made me feel safer and..." he frowned, "maybe vindicated? Like what they were doing to me was wrong in some way?"

Reaching out and touching his arm, I waited until Logan looked at me. "What they were doing was wrong. Period. You did nothing to deserve their treatment. Nothing you could ever do would make you deserve to be harmed in any way. Nothing. Ever. Period." I brushed a thumb over Logan's cheek and wished I could tell if he believed me. All I got was a brief nod as he closed his eyes and leaned into my touch. "But the police will keep us updated. And if we happen to see the assholes again, we can let the department know."

Logan smiled and let out a whoosh of breath as if

pushing away bad thoughts. I'd noticed in the short time I'd known him that he had his demons, but he'd also adapted some coping skills from what I could tell —and they seemed to be fairly helpful ones, I knew that not all coping mechanisms were healthy. "Are you going with Bev and me to the bank and library?"

His face was so hopeful, I kinda hated to burst his bubble. "No, I've got work to do next door at Jesse's. Then I'll be at the Wishing Well for a while this evening."

Logan pouted, but I saw the glimpse of a smile beneath. "Fine, I guess I'll have to deal with being on my own."

I started to feel bad for leaving him, but then he gave me a shit-eating grin and continued.

"All alone, without my very own elderly person to entertain me."

"Mouthy little shit is what you are. That mouth will get you in trouble one of these days," I growled as I put him in a headlock and he squealed.

"Joking, joking," Logan panted as he squirmed away from me, laughter bubbling from him.

"All joking aside, you've got Bev. Everyone else will probably be in and out most of the day. You won't be alone." I bumped his shoulder. "Plus, I'll see you tonight."

Logan grinned and wrapped his arms around my neck, burying his face against me and breathing deep. "I kinda like knowing that, no matter what goes on during our days, our nights come together here."

With a lot more emotion than I was used to clogging my throat, I ran my hands up and down Logan's back. "Yeah, that's a nice way of looking at it." As badly as I wanted to lift his chin, taste his lips, take hold of his hips and press our bodies together, I brushed a kiss against the top of his head and let him go. "Have fun with Bev. Text..." I frowned. "Shit, we need to get you a phone. Does the one you have work okay? Just needs minutes?"

"Yeah, it's old and nothing flashy, but it works." Logan fished it from his repacked backpack.

"See if Bev will run you somewhere to get a card. You have money for some minutes?"

He nodded. "Yeah, I can get a card for the next month and then see what works best for me later. I know I don't have money coming in yet, but the fact I'm safe and have some jobs lined up makes it easier to spend the little bit of cash I'd saved."

"That makes total sense." I grabbed a piece of paper and scribbled my number on it before tearing off the corner and handing it to him. "Okay, here's my number. Once you're up and running with data and minutes, text me."

Logan smiled and tucked the scrap of paper into the pocket of the new jeans he was wearing. "Thanks." He threw himself at me and pressed a kiss against my cheek. "I'm really glad to be here and so happy to know you. Not because you buy me clothes and sleep with me, but because you're a good person and I needed a lot more good in my life." He kissed my cheek again before resting his forehead against my temple. "Thanks to you, I've found a safe home and friends. I'll never take that for granted."

Knowing I shouldn't, but not able to stop myself, I turned slightly and whispered a light kiss over his ear. "I'm really glad you're here, too."

Logan shivered in my arms and I hated letting him go. "I'll see you later. Have a good day at work." He paused on his way out the door. "Ohhh, if I'm working at the Wishing Well, maybe we can get frisky in the backroom?"

I threw my head back and laughed. "I think you'll be clearing tables—probably only washing dishes until you're twenty-one—and my position is usually at the door checking IDs. No fraternization at work is a good rule to follow."

Logan pursed his lips and rolled his eyes. "Old people are so boring."

Wanting nothing more than to push him to the bed and show him just how non-boring I could be—okay, at least in my imagination—I pushed aside the urge and lunged at him. "Mouthy little shit."

Logan shrieked and laughed as he ran from me.

Bev met us at the bottom of the stairs with a smile on her face. "Cruz, baby, you have a wonderful day at work. Logan, let's go. We've got a lot to do. You have your birth certificate and social security card?"

He groaned. "Hang on, I'll grab them. Some elderly guy distracted me."

I rolled my eyes as he rushed up the stairs.

"You like him," Bev mused.

Starting to protest, then seeing on her face that there was no reason to even try to argue, I nodded with hot cheeks. "I do. I know I shouldn't, but I do."

"No need to worry about shouldn't. The heart knows what it wants. When both hearts want the same, good things happen." Bev patted my arm.

"He's so young."

Bev shrugged. "Age is just a number. Cooper and Jesse are getting along just fine and their age gap is even larger. If you and Logan find something together, don't throw it away because of a perceived wrong based on a measly number."

"We've only known each other a day. How can I

already feel so connected and close to someone I barely know?" I ran a hand through my hair and gripped the back of my neck. "It's like I've known him my whole life even though we just met and that seems kinda weird to me."

"You've not been here long enough to hear many of the stories about my late husband. But my dear Jerry and I met on the first day of our junior year and were married before Christmas. Times were different back then and we wanted to be married before he enlisted. Never once did I regret our short courtship and quick marriage. A lot of busybodies gossiped that I was in the family way—little did they know that I'd never be able to carry children—but it didn't matter to me. I knew the first moment Jerry offered to carry my books that he was the man I'd spend the rest of my life with." Bev wiped a tear. "Don't underestimate the very real power of love at first sight and the advice of trust your gut. If you and Logan both feel it, don't worry about time or breaking the norm. The two of you have nothing to prove to anyone else."

"You really feel that?"

"Cruz, child, I wouldn't say it if I didn't feel it." Bev gave my arm a squeeze. "I do think there's something special between you and Logan, I can feel it. I don't think I'd be saying this to you about just any man, but there's something special about Logan."

As Logan's feet thudded down the stairs, I smiled. "Yeah, I think so, too."

I spent the next few hours working on vehicles in Jesse's shop, loving how I could lose myself in the work. Mechanical things had always come easy to me and I probably had my dad to thank for that. He was an office worker during the day, but evenings and weekends were devoted to tinkering on cars in the garage and he had me by his side as soon as I was able to walk. My fondest memories of my dad were how much he loved my mom and repairing cars in the garage.

The fact that both my parents died while I was locked up killed me; would probably haunt me for the rest of my life. I should have been there. Sometimes I worried that the stress over their only child being in prison was what killed them. They'd been so very good to me. Taking me in when my very young, unwed mother gave me up for adoption. Giving me her family name and doing their best to provide me with food, celebrations, and beliefs of my Mexican heritage so I'd never forget where I came from. Working tirelessly and going without so I could be in the private school instead of the public school overrun with gangs.

And yet, I'd still managed to screw up. I'd thought the friends I was with were good guys. Thought we were just out for a night of innocent fun. I'd known I needed to figure out what to do with my life, but I'd mistakenly figured I had time. I still saw those flashing red and blue lights, felt the bite of the handcuffs on my wrists, and swallowed down shame knowing how upset my parents were about me ending up in prison despite all their best efforts.

Mistakes and bad decisions seemed to be my forte.

What if getting involved with Logan is one of those mistakes?

"Hey, man. You 'bout done there? Want a drink before heading to the bar?" Jesse stood next to the car I was working on with two bottles of water.

"Yeah, I'm done. Will finish her up in the morning once that part comes in." I wiped my hands and accepted the water. "Thanks."

We walked out to the little patio area off to the side between the shop and Jesse's house, next to the fence between his property and Remington Place.

Cooper, Jesse's boyfriend—much younger boyfriend—joined us after helping Hadley, their daughter, into roller skates and safety pads. "I can't imagine falling as hard as she does and just jumping back up. I guess I did when I was a kid, but these days, I'd likely be in bed for a week after a fall on skates." He leaned down to kiss Jesse's head before taking a seat.

"Just think what it would do to me," Jesse said.

"Traction for at least a month," Cooper deadpanned. Then he cocked his head. "I bet we could still figure out ways to get sexy."

Jesse laughed. "I'm in traction and you're wanting sex?"

"What? I'm a young, virile male with a fucking hot silver fox boyfriend. As long as you can get it up, I'll ride," Cooper teased.

I laughed. Cooper had no filter, something I'd learned quickly upon moving in and becoming part of the Remington Place family.

Taking Cooper's hand, Jesse turned his attention toward me. "See what I have to put up with?"

"What? Don't act like you don't love me. I keep you young." Cooper swatted at Jesse. "Plus, don't go scaring Cruz off young guys." He winked. "I think he's caught the eye of our very own young Logan."

I groaned and took a long swallow of water.

"Am I wrong?" Cooper asked, batting his lashes.

"Can I be honest?" I asked.

Jesse nodded and Cooper leaned in and patted my knee. "Of course, what's up?"

"I can't believe I'm even saying this because it's crazy, but I like him so much. How can I feel this way for someone I just met? And someone so young?" I ran a hand over my face.

Jesse laughed. "Believe me, I get it. Try being twenty-five years older than the object of your affection and trying your best not to fall for him but being helpless to stop it."

"Aww, that's so sweet. I'm glad to know you're only with me because you're powerless and old," Cooper teased. He turned to me. "Logan is young, but you're not exactly ancient. Fifteen-year difference? That's not much. My advice, after living through it and simply being a fabulous gay man, is to just go with it. Don't worry about the age thing. Do you two feel the same? Enjoy spending time together? Make each other happy? If yes, don't let anything stand in your way."

Taking a swig of water, I hesitated for a moment. What the hell, these were my friends, my chosen family, I could be honest with them. "I've known I was gay since I was a lot younger, but never acted on it for multiple reasons depending on the time period of my life. What if I'm not the man for Logan because I have no clue what I'm doing?"

"You're attracted to him?"

I nodded.

"It's not like there's some huge secret to sex with a man; it's pretty natural. Just do what feels right." Cooper cocked his head. "I get the feeling that Logan may be learning right along with you?"

I rubbed the bridge of my nose. "It's not my place to divulge details, Logan will do that if and when he's ready, but he's had a really shitty past."

Cooper and Jesse winced but nodded. "We'll be here if he ever wants to talk," Jesse said and I believed him. How in the hell had I ended up with such amazing people in my life?

I sighed. "What if he's just interested in me because I stepped in with those assholes in the alley? What if I'm just convenient? I know he needs friends and support, and I want to keep him protected and make him feel safe and wanted, but maybe it's a mistake to let things go any further?"

"Does Logan want to take things further?" Jesse asked.

"I think right now, he just wants a friend and cuddle buddy, but he's pretty affectionate." I frowned. "If things are to move past friends only, he'll have to be the one to initiate and control because of his past."

"Do you want it to go past friends?" Cooper asked.

A rush of heat filled my cheeks and I thought of

Logan in my bed and all the things we could have fun doing.

Jesse chuckled.

"Well, that blush certainly answers that," Cooper teased. "Look, you're both grownups. Logan is younger, but if he's had a rough past he's likely a bit more mature than others his age in some ways—as much as it sucks to think of why he's that way. Be there as his friend and, as long as you're in agreement, let him call the shots if he wants to take it further."

"What if I'm just a convenient cuddle buddy? Would he even like me if not for me stopping him from getting the shit beat out of him?" I leaned my elbows on my knees. "For real, the shit this kid has lived through...and I doubt I even know all of it..." I shuddered and shook my head. "I just don't want him getting involved in something with me if it's not what's best for him."

Cooper smiled softly. "Wouldn't it be nice if we could protect the ones we love and care about from all the painful mistakes in life? But, just like Hadley on her skates, the best thing we can do is give them the right equipment and be there to help them up when they fall. No matter what happens with you and Logan, he needs a supportive friend and I'd say he's lucky to have found that with you."

"I guess I just worry that adding sex to the mix will cause problems." I screwed the lid onto my empty water bottle.

Cooper shrugged. "Then don't add sex to the mix."

I huffed. "Have you seen him? Pretty sure all it would take is one word from his pretty little mouth and I'll be putty in his hands."

Jesse chuckled. "Man, I soooo understand." He tossed his bottle into the recycle bin and reached out to grab his daughter around the waist as she skated by. "I agree with something Bev once told me, though. We may not understand at the time, and bad shit doesn't always have a reason—sometimes it's just bad shit that we can't control or change—but I think people are brought into our lives at just the right time. Maybe you and Logan need each other right now. For a month or so? Longer? Forever? Who knows. Just enjoy the connection and see where it goes." Hadley giggled as Jesse tickled her before letting her return to her fun. "You think Logan would be willing to see Alicia?"

I blew out a long breath. "Maybe? He balked when I first mentioned her because he doesn't have insurance or money. But I told him she uses a sliding pay scale. Maybe once he has some money coming in and some insurance, he'd be more interested?"

"She's really good." Jesse stood. "Helped me more than I can even begin to say; never going to be over losing my wife and daughter, but I'm in a much better place these days."

"She is good. I think Spencer and Rai work with her, too." Cooper checked his phone. "Hadley, come tell Dad bye for now, he's got work."

Hadley made her way to Jesse and launched herself into his arms. "Bye, Dad, love you. See you tomorrow."

Jesse kissed the top of her head. "You and Daddy be good tonight, yeah? Go to bed when he says."

"Duh, me and Daddy are always good," Hadley said with a giggle as she clamored down to return to skating. "How much minutes, Daddy?"

Cooper smiled. "You can have ten more minutes and then we'll wash up and get supper started."

I stood and tossed my water bottle. "Thanks for the chat. I'll see you at work, boss."

"You want to ride with me or you driving?" Jesse asked as he fished in his pocket for his truck keys. "I'm just going to run inside and wash up real quick."

"Same. Think I'll walk. But maybe take a ride home tonight." I gave a wave and headed toward the house.

After a quick clean up, I headed toward the bar.

The walk didn't provide me with any answers or a clearer head, but it felt good to get some fresh air.

I settled into the routine of my position at the Wishing Well and enjoyed the comfortable socializing, friendly banter, and easy work over the next few hours. By the time I climbed into Jesse's truck, I was tired and beyond ready for bed.

And Logan.

I met Bev in the kitchen as she was heating a mug of warm milk. "Can you take this up to Logan, please?" She handed me a bottle of Gatorade and two pain relief pills.

My heart leaped into my throat. "Why? What's wrong?"

"We got a lot done, but he was exhausted by the time we got home today and went to bed with a fever and earache. I sent him up with one bottle and medicine and told him to take a warm shower and sleep. It's about time for more pain medicine and since you're on your way up, you can take them." Bev stirred her milk. "I'm going to bed. I know he won't go to the doctor, I've already argued with him. We need to get him set up with insurance sooner rather than later and get him in to see a doctor. He says he gets earaches and sore throats with fevers all the time; sounds like ear infections and tonsillitis to me. Poor boy probably needs to see an ENT about his ears and throat. Until then, we'll just keep him hydrated and comfortable."

"Are those things dangerous? Like can they get worse?" I hated the thought of Logan being sick.

"Both usually go away on their own, but antibiotics can help clear them up quicker. Fever is just the body's way of fighting the infection. As long as the fever isn't super high and he's not in a ton of pain, he'll be okay." Bev patted my cheek. "Keep him comfortable and we'll work on that insurance."

I kissed her cheek. "Sleep tight." Making my way up the stairs, I worried what state I'd find Logan in.

My heart clenched when I opened the door to our room and found him in our bed, curled in a ball and whimpering in pain. "Lo? Hey, hey, it's okay. Here, Bev sent up some medicine." I sat on the edge of the bed and brushed a hand over his forehead. Shit. He was burning up.

SIX

LOGAN

I'D BEEN DEALING with earaches and sore throats
most of my life. I had a memory of my mom saying
she needed to get me to the doctor to see about my
ears, but then they died and my ears became the
least of my problems.

The foster care agency had me see a doctor from
time to time, but it was basically just for treatment
of infections, not an answer to the underlying
problem. One doctor mentioned I likely needed
tubes in my ears and my tonsils removed, but then I
got moved from one house to another and nothing
ever came of it.

There was never any warning that I was getting
sick. I could wake up feeling fine and within twenty
minutes have a fever and feel like I was dying from
the pain in my ears and throat. The two didn't

always come together, but they often tag-teamed me and made me miserable for at least a couple days.

Foster parents usually got angry at me when I'd end up sick, always afraid I'd infect everyone else. Lilly was pissed when I'd come down with a fever and couldn't work. She had connections though, and could usually get some antibiotics for me. She wasn't giving me the medication to help me; she needed me healthy so I could line her pockets.

Ever since getting away from Lilly, I'd had worse and worse ear infections and sore throats. Sometimes they'd last longer than usual, sometimes they'd hurt even worse than usual, but they'd eventually go away on their own. Last time I'd been sick, something in my ear had popped. The pain had brought me to my knees, but after the initial agony, my ear drained and felt much better. I dreaded the thought of going through that pain again, but I longed for the relief it would bring. The way my ear was throbbing, I had a feeling I knew where things were heading.

As I curled into myself on the bed and cried, the door opened.

"Lo? Hey, hey, it's okay. Here, Bev sent up some medicine."

Cruz.

I'd known Bev and the others would take care of

me, but warmth flooded through me knowing Cruz was there.

He sat on the edge of the bed and brushed a hand over my head.

I sighed in relief and tried to sit up.

"Go slow. Let's get these pills in you and as much Gatorade as you can drink." Cruz helped prop me up so I could swallow the pills—which felt like razor blades going down—and encouraged me to drink more liquid. "Did the shower help? Do you want another one?"

I shivered against the fever. "It felt good, but everything hurts so bad right now, I can't get up. I'm freezing and I just need to lay here."

"Okay, I'm going to shower, I stink from work. I'll be back in a bit and I'll warm you up." Cruz ran a hand over my forehead again. "You good for a little bit?"

Nodding, I curled into a tighter ball and prayed the pain relievers would help soon. The first dose had taken the edge off, they just didn't last very long.

I eventually dozed, grateful that the worst of the pain eased a bit.

Later, minutes or hours, I wasn't sure—but since the pain was slightly less, I figured it hadn't been too long—the bed dipped as Cruz crawled under the covers.

"You okay? Can I hold you?" His big hand on my arm probably should have felt warm, but the fever was still raging so I only knew he'd touched me from the pressure of his skin against mine.

"Don't want to get you sick." I tried to scoot closer to the wall. "I can take the couch."

He huffed and wrapped an arm around me, pulling me close to his hard body. "One, I'm not a doctor, but I don't think ear infections are contagious. Two, I don't have my tonsils, so I maybe can't even get what you have."

"Might be strep, you could still get sick." My protest was weak as I sank into his touch.

"I'll chance it." He brushed his lips over my ear. "Not like we're swapping spit or anything. Just sleep."

"It hurts so bad." I whimpered, trying to position my head so the most painful ear would stop throbbing.

"I'm so sorry. You've got to get insurance and see a doctor. Bev says you get sick like this a lot?"

Nodding, I snuggled deeper into Cruz's arms. "Yeah, it will go away, just sucks until it does."

"Well, I'm going to keep at you about seeing a doctor. You can't deal with this over and over. You seem absolutely miserable." Cruz tightened his arm around me.

"I don't want it to because it will be pure torture, but I think my ear drum burst last time."

"Oh my God," Cruz whispered. "No, no, no, please tell me you'll see a doctor."

"I'm just saying, it might happen and it sucks, but I'll be honest that after the worst of it, the pain at least went away a bit." I took his hand and held it against my chest. "Just warning you so if I scream, you'll know what happened. Or what I think the pain means. There was a loud pop, extreme pain that dropped me, and then my ear poured a bunch of junk and the pain eased a bit." Shrugging, I tried to prevent the yawn wanting to escape for fear it would hurt my ears or throat or both. "Made sense that something burst."

Cruz groaned. "Okay, so I'm just learning this, but it seems I don't handle the pain of others very well because I think I may get sick to my stomach just thinking about that happening. What should I do if it happens?"

I hadn't intended to freak him out, and I didn't want him to feel sick, but having someone care about my well-being was new and very welcome. "Last time, I just used tissue to wipe it up and stuck a cotton ball in my ear. I'm dreading it because it hurts, but honestly, I might welcome the relief."

"Oh God, Logan, I might pass out. Maybe I should go get Bev?"

Chuckling, I squeezed his hand. "It might not even happen. Sorry, didn't mean to make you sick. Please don't leave."

"I may have to get you more pain pills."

I tugged his arms tighter around me. "Not now."

Sometime later, I sat up and groaned. I'd missed the main relief of the pain medication while I slept and the throbbing in my ears was back.

"Lo? What's wrong?" Cruz grumbled as I shifted on the bed.

"Gotta pee. What time is it? Can I have more medicine?"

Cruz reached for his phone. "Yeah, it's been over four hours. You go pee, I'll get more pills. I'll bring another dose for later."

Shivering and wondering if this was what death felt like, I shuffled to the bathroom while Cruz made his way downstairs.

Once I was back in bed, teeth chattering—clearly, the fever hadn't broken yet—I heard voices outside the bedroom.

The door opened and Rai popped his head in. "Hey man, if it gets worse, holler at me. Or even Dre or Khi. Maybe not a whole lot we can actually do, but we're here if you need us."

"Thanks," I muttered, grateful for a nursing student and two first responders in the house. All I wanted to do was sleep and make the pain go away. I honestly understood how people with chronic pain got addicted to pain pills; I probably would have taken whatever was available if it was handed to me and promised relief from the agony.

Cruz handed me two pills and an open bottle of Gatorade. "Maybe we should try the walk-in clinic? Get some antibiotics?"

I shook my head and worked to swallow the pills without crying. "No, not happening. The one time I tried a place like that, they wouldn't treat me because I couldn't provide insurance or an address."

"You've got an address now."

"That's just a place for them to send bills. Maybe I'll consider a doctor once I have insurance—but I don't even know that I'll be able to get insurance. I've lived through this before, I'll..." I paused as my ear crackled and pulsed, then screamed as an intense pain washed over me.

"Fuck." Cruz took the bottle from my hands. "What's wrong? What's happening?"

Doubled over, hand to my ear, I panted as the intensity ebbed a bit. "I think it just busted." Pulling my hand away from my ear, I grimaced at the wetness on my skin. "Can you get a tissue and cotton ball?"

Looking a bit green, Cruz rushed out of the room and returned with the box of tissues and a cotton ball. "What do you need me to do?"

Taking short breaths, I closed my eyes and assessed my pain. "My throat still hurts, and my right ear is painful, but the left one popped and is much better." I took a tissue and wiped away the fluid still pouring from my ear. "Yuck, this is gross. You don't look so good, maybe you shouldn't look at it."

Cruz went from green to gray before turning his back to me and leaning his head between his knees. "Oh God, it's not so much the gross factor, more that I can't stand the thought of you being in pain."

I tried to smile. "Awww, that's actually super sweet. But, for real, this ear was the one hurting the worst and it's so much better now." I wiped away the rest of the liquid and gently stuck the cotton ball in my ear.

"Yeah, but a busted eardrum can't be good." Cruz grabbed a trashcan and helped me throw away all the tissues. "You are going to a doctor. You might be able to do this over and over, but there's no way I'll make it through this again."

"I thought the elderly were usually made of hardier stock."

Cruz gaped. "Oh, you must be feeling better if you've got jokes again." He handed me the Gatorade. "Your fever hasn't broken yet, you mouthy little shit. Drink more and sleep."

"Doctor's orders?" I took as many swigs of the Gatorade as my throat could stand.

"Cruz's orders."

Handing him the bottle and cuddling under the blanket, I laughed and waited until Cruz turned back toward me and took me in his arms. "Who knew I liked bossy older men with a penchant for fainting?"

He growled, the sound rumbling from his chest and doing crazy things to me—things I often wondered if I was capable of feeling—things I likely had no business feeling while I was sick. "I didn't actually faint."

"You were close," I assured him. "I thought I'd have to have Dre bring the smelling salts."

"Whatever," Cruz grumbled. "Go to sleep."

The next time I woke, I was a sweaty mess and I knew the fever had broken.

"You need more medicine?" Cruz mumbled, only half awake.

"I need to pee, take more meds, and a shower." I

squirmed. "Eeww, I feel gross. I'm sorry, I think I got you all sweaty."

Cruz chuckled and ran a hand over my forehead. "I think the fever is gone. How do you feel?"

"Throat is still sore, but better. One ear is fine, but muffled. The other one hurts, but not as bad." I sat up. "I think I'm headed toward being better."

"It's still really early. Maybe you should sleep some more?"

I made a face. "I'm soaked in sweat. I need a warm shower."

"Okay, you go shower. I'll change the sheets and my clothes, then you need to sleep more." Cruz didn't give me any room to argue.

"Bossy old man," I muttered.

"Mouthy little shit," he shot back with a smile and a wink.

"You want to shower with me?" I bit my lip. I wasn't even sure I'd be comfortable with it, and I figured I was pressing my luck, but it was fun to see Cruz squirm a bit.

"Not that I don't want to, but I think you'd be better off just washing quickly and getting some more rest." The tips of his ears were pink and I couldn't help but adore him a bit more with each passing minute.

"You're not going to shower?" I plucked the damp shirt away from his chest.

"Nah, I'll just change. I didn't get sweaty, just my clothes. I'll shower in the morning." He gave me the nearly empty Gatorade bottle. "Here, take the medicine and get your shower."

By the time I'd brushed my teeth and showered and felt almost human, I made my way back to the bedroom. The shower had exhausted me, but the warm, dry clothes were worth it. True to his word, Cruz had changed the sheets and ushered me into bed.

"I'm tired, but not at all sleepy," I complained as I settled into his warm arms again.

"You need a bedtime story?" he teased.

"Yes, tell me about little Cruz." I snorted. "And I mean Cruz as a child, that was not an innuendo about your dick."

Cruz laughed out loud. "Yeah, I got that. If you were referring to my dick as Little Cruz I think I'd need to be offended."

"Those gray sweatpants you had on earlier hid nothing—little isn't a word I'd use." I snuggled closer. "Come on, story time. You said you had your tonsils out? Was it terrible?"

"Definitely wouldn't tell you if it was." His words

held a smile. "I was a toddler, maybe a bit older, three or four? I had tubes put in, adenoids and tonsils removed. I don't remember it much, but I recall my mom laughing at how I bounced right back and the tubes did wonders for the ear infections I was prone to."

"What were you like as a kid?"

"Quiet. Always trying to blend in. Torn between wanting to fit in with the other kids in my very white school and wanting to know where I came from, be true to my Mexican heritage." His thumb caressed the back of my hand.

"Do you still feel that way?"

"Not so much on the fitting in part. I used to work so hard to find my place between where I came from and where I was, but prison and the eight years since kinda changed all that."

I squeezed his hand. "What do you mean?"

He shrugged against my back. "Figured out quickly that I don't really fit, but these last eight years have shown me it doesn't really matter. Being here, just this short amount of time, has helped me see that I don't have to fit in, it's okay to just be me. It's okay to hold on to my Mexican heritage. It's okay to hold on to the past that my parents gave me. It's okay to be gay. It's okay that I'm thirty-five and feel like I'm just now, for the first time in my life, finding myself."

"I like that. Gives me hope that maybe I can get my own shit figured out." I pulled his hand to my mouth and kissed his knuckles. "Things have been a nightmare for so long, it's kinda hard to believe that I can relax and breathe now. The demons in my head are still telling me I'm not worth the time or effort, that this is all too good to be true and people will still hurt me, but my heart feels so much here, it's hard to not let myself think that maybe this is when things start going right." My heavy eyes drooped.

"Maybe we both get our happy ending here. I like that idea." Cruz's breath whispered over my ear.

"I'm a bit too wiped out for a happy ending, old man," I teased.

"Oh my God, how do you turn everything into something sexual?" Cruz chuckled. "That's not what I meant."

I smiled sadly. "I know." After a heartbeat, I went on. "I think it's kinda a way to protect myself. Sex has two spots in my brain. One side is all the bad stuff and I think I joke and make brash comments to try to hide how badly it's all hurt me."

Cruz's arm tightened around me. "What's the other side?" His words were a gruff mixture of sadness, worry, and protectiveness, like he wanted to save me from my past.

"The hopeful side. Hope that I'm not broken.

Hope that the fantasies I have in my head can actually be brought to life." I paused for a moment. "Sometimes I worry that there's something wrong with me—how can I live through all that horrible stuff and still have these wants and desires? But, on the flip side, I feel lucky that maybe I can push all the bad shit aside and end up having a normal, healthy love life." I took a long breath and blew it out slowly. "I want that, to be normal."

"I think I'm way too tired for this to make much sense, but overall, I think I get it. Normal is overrated, but I get wanting to feel it. The problem comes when you start thinking your normal has to match someone else's. We're all different, all unique, and we have very different normals." He threaded our fingers together. "I think it's good you can have desires and fantasies separate from the bad shit. But I also wonder if it's better to push aside and ignore the bad shit or if you should work through it. I'm not a professional, but it worries me that just ignoring it means that maybe it builds up bigger and bigger and one day it's just too much." He kissed the top of my head. "I won't push—much—but I really think it would be good for you to talk to Alicia. Or at least to someone."

My heartbeat doubled. "In my heart, I know you're right. But my head is screaming no.

Unpacking all those tightly packed and hidden away terrors scares the shit out of me. Ignoring them and moving on with good things sounds much more enjoyable. Like, why do I need to relive the nightmares? Can't I just explore a healthy sex life and find happiness?"

Cruz was quiet for a moment. "But if those things still lurk, hidden in the shadows, can you ever really be happy?"

I tensed. "Do you think the shit I was made to do will just go away? The shit that was done to me will ever go away? Hidden away or not, talked to death on a shrink's couch or not, they will always be there," my words caught in my throat.

"I'm sorry, I didn't mean to upset you. I get what you're saying and I think I can empathize with your fears. You have to do what you think is best for you. We'll be here, no matter what."

"What if I talk to someone and they make me work through the bad shit and it ruins me? Right now, I have hope that someone can find me desirable. What if it all comes out and I can't get past it? Can't ever bring myself to explore within a happy, healthy relationship?" I shuddered in Cruz's arms, my head and heart screaming at me to shut down and sleep, to ignore the hard parts.

"What if talking about it frees you in ways you

didn't know were possible?" Cruz ran his fingers up and down my arm. "You are gorgeous, inside and out. No matter your past—whether you tell me about it or not, whether you talk to a professional about it or not—I'm crazy attracted to you and want to do whatever you're comfortable with whenever you say the word. But even if that time never comes, I'm here."

"Is that really fair to you? If I can never do an intimate relationship, is it fair to ask you to be here for me? I can't expect you to just put your life on hold and deal with my crazy shit."

"Hey, I think maybe we've talked this to death right now. You're still sick. We're both tired." He brushed a kiss along the shell of my ear. "What we've got here is more than I've had in my entire life and I'm pretty damn satisfied with it. No pressure to go further. Let's sleep and we'll take things one day at a time, yeah?"

Squeezing the tears from my eyes, I nodded and sniffled. "Yeah, I'm probably not in the best state of mind to be delving deep right now. Sleep sounds good."

"You need anything? Drink? Bathroom?"

I shook my head. A few moments later, I whispered, "Cruz?"

"Hmmm?"

"When I'm better and once I get settled in with a job or two, there are a few things I think I need to do."

He waited and just held me close.

"I think I need to get some insurance and see a doctor."

"I agree."

I took a deep breath. "I think I should probably talk to someone. This Alicia lady seems like a good place to start."

His body relaxed slightly. "I agree and I'll help in whatever way you need me to."

Hugging his arm close to my chest, I continued, "And I think I need to kiss you."

Cruz's breathing paused and, for a moment, I worried I'd said the wrong thing.

But then he chuckled and kissed the back of my neck. "I agree."

I fell asleep with a smile on my face. Sure, I was still sick and I had a shit ton of life to work through, but I was safe. I had shelter, probable jobs, food, and friends. I had Cruz. Definitely things worth smiling about.

SEVEN

CRUZ

OVER THE NEXT month or so, Logan settled in quickly at Remington Place and he brought a lot to our little crew. For someone who had such a shitty past, it was amazing how caring, empathetic, and willing to help others he was. He could have—and would have had every right to—turned in on himself, lashed out, given as much hurt to others as was given to him, but he didn't.

Instead, he spent his days happily juggling four different jobs and itching to figure out times he could volunteer at the homeless shelter.

"That place and so many like it were my saving grace for three years after I got away from Lilly, I want to give back," Logan had told me when I indicated maybe he was busy enough already.

Logan and I had a unique and extremely close

relationship. He was fiercely loyal to me, almost to a fault, and I often wondered what the hell I ever did to deserve him. We spent every single night wrapped in each other's arms. Kisses to hands, cheeks, necks, and temples were completely the norm, but no actual mouth kissing—despite how badly I longed to taste him.

And Logan had wriggled his pretty little ass against me in bed enough times that I knew he felt how hard I got for him. More than once, he'd pressed his stiff length against my thigh, but never anything more.

All of that was okay with me.

And all of that was driving me insane.

I knew things had to move at Logan's pace and he may never be ready to go further. I was truly okay with it. What he and I shared—whatever the crazy friendship-plus-more connection we had going on—I enjoyed every moment with him. He was giving me something I'd never had before and part of me appreciated the chance to savor it and move slowly.

The other part of me spent much too long jacking off in the shower ever since Logan came to stay.

"Can we go throw pennies in the wishing well?" Hadley asked as Logan and I walked with her through the park. "I made a wish for my Dad and Daddy and it came true. Now I'm going to wish for a baby monkey." Her eyes grew wide and she slapped a hand over her mouth. "Oh no, I said it out loud, now it won't come true!"

I laughed. "How 'bout we pretend we didn't hear it and you can make all the wishes in the world for a baby monkey."

"And it needs to be a real baby monkey. Daddy got me a stuffed one, but I want a live one." Hadley hopped along, jumping over cracks in the sidewalk, as we neared the wishing well fountain.

Logan had asked me to take him to his ENT appointment and Jesse needed Hadley picked up from school, so we'd walked to the school to get Hadley before dropping her at Jesse's and then heading to the ENT.

"I think I've got some money," I said and dug in my pocket.

"Thank you!" Hadley skipped off to the wishing well with Logan and I close behind. She was nearing eight-years-old, super smart, well-behaved, and fun to be around—definitely ruined me for other kids because now I figured all would be the same. Cooper had laughed and told me to come to her next birthday party and see just how wrong I was.

When we caught up with Hadley, we watched as she carefully chose her tossing spots, closed her eyes and clenched the coin to her chest, kissed her hand,

and then let the money fly. She did this for each separate piece of change.

"I'm sure I did, but I don't ever remember making wishes in a wishing well," Logan mused. "Even if I did, I'm sure I wasn't wishing for don't let my parents die, don't let me end up sexually abused. If I did, those wishes definitely didn't work."

I put my arm around him and kissed the top of his head. "Tell me some of your wishes. No coins, just what you wish now."

Logan leaned into me as we watched Hadley. "Part of me feels that wishes are worthless—either make them happen or let them go."

"Come on, humor me."

He sighed. "I wish my past had been different, but it hurts too much to dwell on things I can't control or change, so I'm trying to focus on the present and what I can control."

I smiled into his hair. He'd had two meetings with Alicia and seemed to really like her. It was good to hear him using what he learned from her. I had a feeling his work with Alicia would get harder and heavier long before it got better, but Logan had a fire in him that made me think he'd make it through.

"I wish I could have had a regular teen experience. Hanging out with friends, birthday

parties, school events, first dates, that kind of stuff."
Logan shrugged against me.

My heart hurt for my sweet, fierce boy who had
missed out on so much, been through so much, yet
still managed to bring so much joy to those around
him. "You never had a birthday party?"

He was quiet for a moment. "I can remember
family birthday parties, but never any friend ones. A
lot of things around my parents' death are a blur, but
I remember that I was supposed to have a friend
party for my eleventh birthday, but they died and it
never happened." He pushed a pebble with the toe of
his shoe.

"When is your birthday?"

"Months away. November third. I'll be twenty-
one."

I tucked all of Logan's wishes away for when I
had more time to think them through and form a
plan. "Fourteen years difference doesn't really sound
any better than fifteen years," I grumbled.

Logan turned slightly, his front pressing into my
side. "I know we joke about age…"

I raised a brow.

"Okay, I joke about age," he amended with a
smile. "But you have to know our ages mean nothing
to me. It's fun to poke at the old guy," he bit his lip,

"but it's all in fun. You don't seem old to me. You're just Cruz."

With a smile, I gripped the back of his neck and pulled him close, pressing a kiss to his forehead. "And you're just Logan. A mouthy little shit who likes to give me a rough time, but I wouldn't trade you."

"Not even for a baby monkey?" Logan tossed his head toward Hadley. She had to be running out of coins soon.

I laughed. "Definitely not for a baby monkey."

Once we dropped Hadley off at Jesse's place, we climbed in the car and headed toward the ENT.

"How's your schedule looking for the week?" I asked. With four jobs, he'd struggled in the beginning to get all of his hours to line up.

"Good. I think I've finally gotten into a routine and we've set some hours at each place, so it's working a lot better than in the beginning."

He spent a couple hours a day at the Wishing Well, mostly washing dishes and clearing tables. Once he was twenty-one, he wanted to look into serving or working the bar.

The position at Cooper's preschool was the most flexible. Logan went in after hours and on weekends to refill supplies and organize.

He seemed to really like the quiet hours he spent at the library. He did a couple hours a day there, checking in and re-shelving books. Ever since he'd gotten his library card—which had been more as documentation for his state ID, but had turned out to be something he really enjoyed—he'd brought book after book home and spent a lot of his free time reading.

Of all his part-time work, Logan loved the animal shelter the most. His hours there varied between mornings and evenings, but his responsibilities were usually the same. He cleaned cages and played with the animals. The kid was head-over-heels for the puppies and dogs, but it was the cats that really caught his heart. I had a feeling he'd be asking Bev to bring some kittens home sooner rather than later.

"Thanks for coming with me today," Logan said as he stared out the window. "Don't know why I'm so nervous."

"No problem. It was nice to have the time off. We should walk to the park more often."

Logan smiled. "You have two jobs and I have four. I guess we could plan three a.m. park walks."

"True, we're busy. But we can't forget to take time out." I pulled into the parking lot for the ENT office. "Do you want me to come in with you?"

Logan shot me a look. "Yes? Please. Unless you don't want to?"

"It's fine. Just didn't want to overstep." We climbed from the car and made our way into the office.

"You'll come with me to talk to the doctor too?" Logan bounced his knee after he'd checked in and taken a seat.

"If that's what you want."

"I do."

When the nurse called Logan's name, we both stood and she shot us a look.

"He's coming with me to make sure I get all the information. I want him with me," Logan said, chin lifted and challenge in his voice.

"Not a problem, Mr. Miles. We're going to be in the third room on the right," the nurse said with a friendly smile.

An hour later, I took Logan's shaking hand as we walked to the parking lot. "You okay?"

He nodded mutely.

I had a feeling he wasn't okay.

In two weeks, he'd go in for a routine tonsillectomy, adenoidectomy, and placement of tubes in his ears—but it was still surgery and he was shaken. The doctor said Logan's tonsils were scarred and the chronic infections would only cause further problems if not removed. His adenoids were enlarged; not causing a ton of problems—which seemed to surprise the doctor—but had no reason to remain.

Logan's ears were the biggest issues. They were so full of glue-like build-up—from years and years of ear infections and inability to drain properly—that the doctor was actually surprised Logan didn't have poor hearing and more constant infections. The ear drum that had busted was healing well, but the doctor wanted tubes in to help with the drainage as soon as possible.

"I'll go with you. It's on a Friday and he said you'll likely be back to work by Wednesday, if not sooner." The doctor had also said the surgery was more difficult to recover from the older a person got, but I didn't mention that. "It's going to be so great to not have to worry about being sick. Plus, he said you'll probably be shocked by how much better you'll hear." I squeezed his hand over the console. "Leave the hearing aids to the old man," I teased.

Logan smiled. "Just nervous. I've never had surgery. Seeing a therapist, going to the doctor, having an income and a safe place to stay, all of these things are new and happening quickly. They aren't bad, just a lot to take in." He closed his eyes and leaned his head back. "I think sometimes, when things move so fast, I get worried that I'm being duped or steamrolled like with Lilly. She had me trapped long before I realized what was going on and it's scary; what if I'm getting in way over my head again?"

I ran his words through my head. "Yeah, I can see that fear. But, if you stop and think about each new thing happening to you, they're all positives and for the best in the long run."

He scoffed. "Lilly was good in the beginning, too. How can I tell the difference?"

Reaching for his hand, I gave it a squeeze. "Because you've got an amazing brain in that pretty head of yours. Lilly was superficially good—plying you with material items you wanted and needed, taking advantage of a young kid with a heavy past." I put on my turn signal and waited for a light to change. "These things you're dealing with right now? They didn't come looking for you, they aren't taking advantage of you. They're tools and services for you to use and make the best of. If you feel used or overwhelmed or taken advantage of in any of the situations, you simply walk; you're not tethered to any of it, not trapped."

Logan was quiet for a moment, but his hand relaxed in mine and I heard his breathing slow. "Yeah, I like looking at it that way. Have you been to therapy or something? That sounded very expert-ish."

I laughed. "We had therapy sessions in prison. But there was also a month-long series on Cognitive Reframing and it provided some good tips on how to rethink situations and see them as positives or challenges rather than negatives."

He wrinkled his nose. "I wonder if Alicia will make me do that? Don't get me wrong, what you said was helpful and I like that way of looking at it, I'm just not sure I want to reframe every bit of my past."

I shrugged. "I don't think it's about reframing everything. But I've found it helpful when regrets from my past are getting to me or if I'm feeling a lot of anxiety about present issues."

Logan glanced at me. "Was it hard after you got out of prison?"

I nodded. "For sure. I'd lost my parents, had no home to return to, and had a prison record. For the first year, I couldn't leave the area because of needing to meet with my parole officer. When I was released from that duty, I decided a fresh start was for the best. Trying to get a job when you've been in prison is difficult. Very few people want to take a chance. Housing, employment, all of it is hard when that hangs over your head. I wandered aimlessly for what seemed like eternity." I gave him a smile. "Then I found myself here. Jesse was a God-send offering me a job doing something I fucking love. Bev is my savior. The crew—being loved and welcomed and supported—they're what I'd been missing. I think for the first time in my life, I feel actual contentment."

"Yeah, finding Remington and all of you definitely sent my spiral into more of a defined path with a purpose." He frowned. "If that even makes sense."

"It does, I get what you're saying." With another squeeze to his hand, I went on, "But you're okay with having the surgery? I think it's good to get it done sooner rather than later, but you're in control with that, you make the call. I'm sure they can schedule it further down the line." I didn't want him to feel like he was being forced into anything.

"Yeah, I'm good with it. If it means never having to go through the pain again, definitely." Logan opened one of the pamphlets the nurse had provided. "So weird to think that ear infections will still happen, but they'll drain like normal rather than cause all the pain."

"It'll be nice having a doctor to call for medication, too."

Once we got home, we sat with Bev and explained all Logan had learned at the appointment.

"Warm soup and cold ice cream all that

weekend," Bev said with a wink. "We'll take care of you and get you on your feet."

A bit later, the entire crew made their way to the kitchen—Jesse, Cooper, and Hadley bustled through the backdoor—and a comfortable buzz filled the room. People laughed and talked as they filled their plates and made their way to the large table.

Bev always took the same seat, the rest of the chairs got filled by whoever landed in them first. A tense hush came over the table when Dre and Khi came to the table and realized the only two remaining seats were next to each other.

"Well now, I'm gonna go out on a limb and guess that neither of you boys have cooties so sit your bottoms in those chairs so we can say grace and eat. I didn't spend all that time cooking to have it get cold because the two of you want to continue your little squabble." Bev gestured toward the chairs with a look on her face that left zero room for argument.

Dre and Khi plopped down, both disgruntled, out of sorts, and tense if their faces and body language were anything to go on.

Bev offered a quick grace and everyone dug in to the amazing food.

As friendly, casual conversation and the clink of silverware danced through the air, a battle brewed across the table from me and I couldn't help but fight a smile.

Dre—gorgeous, creative, sometimes pensive, always ready to help or offer a friendly smile—was a lefty. Khi—sinfully handsome, broody, sometimes withdrawn, perhaps a bit intimidating—was right handed. Their seats at the table put them closer together than I'd ever seen them and their elbows clashed with each and every bite.

Dre pushed his long braids over his shoulder with a huff before jabbing with his elbow and forking a bite to his mouth.

Khi clanked his knife down harder than necessary and grunted before doing his own elbow defense as he took a bite of porkchop.

The two were so embroiled in their elbow battle, they hadn't noticed the entire table had gone quiet as we bit back smiles and watched the two grown men elbow each other, grunt and huff like annoyed cavemen, and eat a meal they couldn't possibly be enjoying.

Eventually, Bev steepled her fingers under her chin and cleared her throat. "I guess we should ask Cooper, the preschool teacher, what he'd suggest for dealing with this little altercation."

Dre and Khi continued their meal, more intent on

poking and prodding and casting daggers than anything else.

Bev cleared her throat again and Hadley giggled.

Dre and Khi finally looked up.

"If you boys are going to act like bratty, spoiled children, maybe you should leave the table." Bev cocked a brow at her nephew and Khi.

"He's..." Dre started, but clamped his mouth shut when Bev shot him a look.

"They should just switch places," Hadley piped up. "And if we had a friend bench, they could sit on it and talk about their problems."

A few snorts and chuckles sounded around the table as Dre and Khi gritted their teeth and clenched their fists.

"Well, gentlemen, what will it be? Switch places or leave the table?" Bev was clearly out of patience.

Khi shrugged a shoulder and pushed back from the table. "Thank you for dinner, ma'am. I need to get to bed, early shift." He gathered his plate and silverware, shoveling a couple more bites into his mouth, and took care of his dishes at the sink.

Everyone returned to eating, a slight awkwardness—whether from the tension or the absurdity of the scene—over the table.

Dre waited until Khi had left the room before he took a final bite and stood. "Dinner was delicious as always, Aunt Bev. I need to get ready for my shift." He deposited his dishes in the sink before kissing his aunt's cheek. "See you tomorrow."

He thundered up the stairs.

"They're either going to eventually kill each other or give in to that fiery tension brewing between them," Raiden said with a smirk.

"Mmhm," Bev hummed. "I know which one I'm hoping for, but I fear there may be violence before all is said and done."

"Never a dull moment around here." Jesse chuckled.

"That, my boy, is the damn truth." Bev stood. "Now, who wants dessert?"

Later, curled up in our bed, after showers and watching a few episodes of a drama Logan liked on Netflix, I worked up the nerve to ask him something I'd been thinking about all day.

Just as I began to speak, Logan yawned and rolled from the bed. "Gonna brush my teeth," he said as he left the room.

When he returned from the bathroom, I stepped in front of him before he could crawl back onto the bed. "Wanted to ask you something." My fingers brushed his elbow and trailed down his arm to lightly grip his hand.

Logan's bright blue eyes sparkled with warmth and curiosity as he smiled and met my gaze.

I cleared my throat. "I don't want to push and I'll understand if you want to say no, maybe it's too soon."

He cocked his head to the side and studied me, waiting patiently while I fumbled through the words.

"I want to be the person to take you on your first date." The words rushed from me and I dipped my head, gripping the back of my neck. "Would be the first time I've dated a guy." I shrugged. "Firsts for both of us."

Logan smiled softly. "I don't need a pity date. I'll get there eventually."

Scowling, I squeezed his hand. "It's not pity, I swear. I know you talked about wishes today, and I do want to give you those things, but me asking you to go on a date with me isn't about that." I ran my hand over my short hair and huffed. "I mean, yes, the idea came from today, but I'm not asking you out of pity. I'm asking you because I love spending time with you and I want to do more of it."

Logan pursed his lips. "So, like a real date? Dinner? Movie? Similar?"

Not able to hold back the grin, I nodded. "Similar. I was thinking dinner but I've got something else in mind instead of a movie. I think it will be fun."

"When?" He wrinkled his nose. "Surgery is in two weeks. Before or after that?"

"I was hoping before. And if you want to wait, that's okay. But we've slept together every night since we met, I figured a quick turnaround on the date wouldn't be too much of an overstep."

"Yes," Logan answered with a smile he couldn't hide even though he tried.

And when I thought the night couldn't get any better, Logan's eyes locked with mine and a thickness filled the air between us. His hand traveled up my arm and trailed over my chest, his eyes never leaving mine, both of our breathing suddenly heavy.

I'd wanted to kiss Logan—really kiss him, not just the casual cheek and head kisses we'd shared—since day one. But I'd convinced myself that he needed time, he needed to be the one controlling anything that happened between us. I'd even gone so far as to think maybe what we had was more platonic on his end than it was on mine.

But the heat in Logan's innocent eyes told me he was feeling the same draw, the same desire, maybe even the same crazy thoughts of love and forever. Seriously, how in the hell did my head and heart go from stepping in to save the kid and offering him a safe place to live to thinking he may be the guy I'd be happy spending the rest of my life with?

The thought was ludicrous, but it also made total sense. Logan and I got along great and loved spending time together. Even without the idea of sex, I had no issues thinking that he could be my forever.

"I really want to kiss you right now," Logan whispered, licking his lips as his eyes dropped to my mouth. "But I'm scared I might be bad at it."

"That's not possible," I answered, surprised at how gruff my voice was. I stepped closer, wrapping my hand around Logan's slender neck and leaning in to nuzzle his ear. "Your decision, your move, but I'm completely on board and there's no way anything between us could be bad. I've held you in my arms, felt your body against mine every damn night and I know how good it feels. Your lips on mine? Tasting you? Never going to be anything bad about that."

Logan whimpered and rubbed his cheek against my face. "I'm scared. I want it so badly, but what if it changes things?"

I pulled back enough to cup his cheek and meet his eyes. "It's your call. But I'd like to think we can move from friends who sleep together and touch to friends who sleep together, touch, and kiss without too much of a problem."

"Kissing is...more intimate? I just don't want to lose what we have."

"Then we don't have to do it." My dick ached and my heart plummeted as I pulled him close and brushed a kiss against his forehead. "Always your call."

I moved to pull down the comforter, but Logan yanked my arm, pulling me close.

"I wasn't done," he quipped and a burst of pride filled my chest at him taking a stand for himself. "I've never felt this way about someone, never felt so close and connected." Logan's mouth was mere millimeters from mine, his breath tickling my lips. "I want things with you I never thought I'd be able to want. The thought of kissing you scares me to death, but the thought of not kissing you is even worse."

Just as I tried to form some semblance of words, Logan moved to press his mouth against mine and I lost the ability to breathe, to think, to do anything other than drown in his kiss.

Instant heat crackled between us, my arms wrapping around his waist as his snaked around my neck. Fighting the urge to push him to the bed, I let Logan lead the kiss. His lips glided across mine, his teeth nipped gently, and his tongue traced the seam of my mouth as if dipping a toe in water.

Opening slightly, I invited him in, but waited for

Logan to make that move on his own. When he did, I couldn't help the gruff groan that escaped when his tongue met mine, slick and hot.

We kissed for several long moments, lost in our shared bliss. Logan's fingers played lazily with the hair at the back of my head, my hands caressed up and down his back, and our lips never broke apart.

When Logan finally stepped back, breathing heavily, eyes wide and shiny, pretty pink lips swollen and wet, he touched a hand to his mouth and smiled. "Wow," he whispered. "That was everything I'd ever imagined kissing could be, but so much more. Thank you."

I pulled him into a hard hug. "You never have to thank me for kissing you, I got just as much from that as you did. Maybe more."

We crawled into bed and settled into our usual big spoon, little spoon arrangement. Logan wiggled into me, getting comfortable, and then he froze.

I knew he felt my rock-hard dick against his ass— wasn't the first time I'd been hard with him in my arms, but following the kiss it seemed like a bigger deal. "Sorry," I mumbled and tried to pull away. Way to go, asshole. Turn a sweet, innocent kiss into something he maybe can't handle.

"Don't be sorry. I'm not afraid of you, I don't feel threatened by you—ever. Knowing I did that to you," he reached back and gripped my hip, pulling me close so my cock nestled between his ass cheeks, "is crazy hot." Logan took my hand and guided it to the front of his pajama bottoms. As my hand brushed over his hard length, he whimpered. "What you do to me. I want you, Cruz. Wanna roll over, strip you naked, and ride you until we both come." He paused, rocking his ass against my erection and his hard-on into my palm. "But I'm scared. Scared I'd shut down. I don't want just sex with you, I want more."

I kissed the back of his neck. "Even I wouldn't agree to going further tonight. This is your show, you call the shots. Only ever kissing? I'll survive."

"Is kissing all you'd want?"

"No, and I'd be doing a lot of jerking off," I teased, "but if it's all you can give, I'll take whatever you're able."

"I want more. I think we can move slowly, a little bit at a time. I'll let you know what I'm comfortable with as we go." He pulled my hand up to his chest. "If you're okay with that?"

"Whatever you need, whatever you want. I'm here, always."

EIGHT

LOGAN

"Does this look okay for a date?" I asked.

Spencer and Rai popped their heads up from the video game they were playing and smiled. "Lookin' good," Spencer said with a wink. "Who's the lucky guy?"

Biting my lip, cheeks hot, I tried to reel it in. "Cruz wanted to take me to dinner and some wreck room thing."

Rai held a hand to his heart. "That's so sweet. I love seeing you two together."

"Nervous?" Spencer cocked his head.

I nodded. "Yeah, it's my first date."

"Ever?" Rai's eyes went wide.

Fighting the urge to feel bad—I knew Rai didn't mean anything by his question—I used what Alicia had taught me. "Yeah, I had a few detours along the way, so certain milestones are a bit further down the line for me." There was so much more to that statement—things I was sure Rai and Spencer weren't ready to hear, even if I had been ready to share—but it was the simple truth. I hadn't had a normal experience so it wasn't surprising I was a bit behind in many aspects.

"We can get that," Rai answered. "Sorry, didn't mean to sound judgmental. I think people who feel different, experience exclusion in one form or another, or have to focus on surviving are understandably going to arrive at certain milestones later than others." He leaned into Spencer and let his boyfriend kiss the top of his head.

My eyes grew wide. Wow, yeah, Rai got it. I smiled softly. "Exactly. I used to feel like a failure for all the things I haven't done, but now I realize that most of it wasn't my fault, I was simply busy surviving, and maybe now I'm at a place where I'm able to start experiencing some of those firsts."

"Have fun," Spencer said. "Let us know about the wreck room place. I've heard of it, sounds like it could be a good time. Smashing shit and tearing up a room? I'm in."

I said goodbye before heading downstairs.

Dre and Bev were in the kitchen. I fixed myself a

glass of water and downed it, hoping to wash away my nerves. No luck.

"You look great," Dre said. He studied my clothing. I'd borrowed everything from Cooper because I had zero dressy clothing and I wanted more than jeans and a hoodie for my first date.

"Thanks, Cooper set me up."

"Next time, come see me. I've got a few pieces I think would be amazing on you. If you give me enough time, I can probably do a few alterations to make sure the fit is perfect." Dre fixed the collar of my shirt and swept a hand down my sleeve.

"Will do. I've not had a lot of time or reason for nice clothes, but I love the idea of putting together outfits." I washed my glass and placed it in the dish drainer.

The first few times I'd fallen prey to Dre studying my clothes or making adjustments to other's outfits, I'd been kinda creeped out and intimidated. However, I soon realized it was just his eye for fashion and creating that had him seeing things differently than most.

Which made it a bit weird when you found yourself confronted by a gorgeous man in a perfect-fit EMT uniform—I was all about Cruz, but damn, those pants hugged Dre's ass just right—eyeing you up and down and talking about colors and fit and design. Dre was a mixed bag and I really liked him. Just took a bit to figure out he wasn't a what-you-see -is-what-you-get type of guy; Dre had multiple facets.

"When are you leaving?" Bev asked.

"He's picking me up at six." I pressed my lips together, trying to suppress the smile fighting to overtake my face.

Cruz had insisted that our first date be as authentic as possible. He'd made sure the day and time worked for both our schedules—which wasn't super easy—and he was getting ready at Jesse's place. He wanted to come to the front door and pick me up like he would have if we didn't share a house, a room, and a bed.

"Well, you boys have fun. I'm heading out to meet Eloise for bingo." Bev bustled around the kitchen. "I left a note about leftovers in the fridge."

"You cook for us almost every night, pretty sure we can all survive on leftovers or carry-out while you play bingo." Dre kissed his aunt's cheek. "I'll be at work over night. Call if you need anything. See you tomorrow." He headed out the back door while Bev went toward her room.

I wandered to the living room. I had about fifteen minutes before Cruz was scheduled to arrive. Maybe it was a bit silly for him to shower and dress at

Coop's house and come to the front door. But my heart swooned with how sweet the gesture was. Sure, we could have just gotten ready in our room and headed out the back door to Cruz's car, but the fact that he wanted to make our date as real as possible meant a lot to me.

"Heard someone has a hot date," a deep, smooth voice said from the doorway.

I turned to find Khi leaned against the door frame with an appraising smile and blushed. "Yeah."

"You look great. Where are you guys going?"

"Thanks. Dinner and that wreck room place over in Hutton."

"Some of my buddies on the crew were talking about that place, sounds fun."

I smoothed my palms down my pants and smiled. "Should be."

Khi was the person in the house I knew the least. I didn't know Dalton and Gabby well, but that was more because I didn't see them much. I saw Khi almost as much as I saw the rest of my housemates, but he was definitely the most intimidating and hardest to get to know. Like he had walls and didn't want to let anyone in. Maybe that was why he and Dre were like oil and water—although, I'd heard they had some sort of past together, but I wasn't aware of the why behind their tension-filled animosity. The fact they'd been put in a room together—by Dre's own aunt, no less—made their extreme dislike for each other more evident. I wasn't sure it could be called hate because they were hardly ever around each other thanks to opposite shifts, but Dre and Khi really didn't mesh well together.

"You and Cruz seem good together," Khi mused.

I didn't try to hide the smile. "He's great."

Khi frowned. "I'm not going to even pretend that I know anything about you, your past, or your current situation, and I'm definitely not trying to offend or hurt or cause a problem."

My hackles rose and I immediately tensed, waiting for something I wasn't going to like. Maybe Dre had a reason for not liking Khi.

"Just don't lose yourself." His eyes darkened and a look of something—regret? Anger? Hurt?—filled his face. "Don't make him your life. Because when he's gone, you're the one left to pull it together and continue on your own. Don't fall so deep in with him that you have no clue who you are when you find yourself alone."

As much as part of me wanted to lash out, tell Khi to mind his own fucking business because what Cruz and I had wasn't like that, I paused and studied him. The man was in pain and he wasn't trying to hurt me, just to save me from what he was going through. I didn't want to think of my life without Cruz and my defenses were up, but I saw past Khi's warning and wondered just what had happened to him.

He broke free from whatever memory had him zoned out and pushed away from the door frame. "Sorry, didn't mean to be a downer. You're a good kid, just don't want to see you make the same mistakes I did." When I started to protest, he held up a hand. "I know our circumstances and histories are completely different—or, I assume they are. Hell, who knows, maybe we have more in common than we think. But make sure you never lose sight of Logan, even when you're deep in the love haze of what you and Cruz have going on." Khi gave a nod. "I gotta go sleep. Ignore me and my rambling ass, for real. I've been on a twenty-four-hour shift and I'm worthless right now. My shit is not your shit." He sighed. "Sorry for being a downer. Have a good time."

Khi turned and plodded up the stairs. Just as I started to let my head examine his words, a knock on the door startled me.

"Let me get it," Bev said, making her way toward the door.

"I thought you were going to bingo?"

"I am. But I wasn't going to miss your first date."

She gave me a wink. "Plus, it gives me a moment to razz Cruz," she whispered before pulling open the door.

Cruz stood there looking fucking edible as he smiled at Bev.

"Come in," Bev said. "Now, just what are your intentions with our young Logan?" She delivered the line almost without breaking a smile.

I snorted, quickly bringing a hand to my mouth to hide my laughter.

Cruz brought a bouquet of flowers from behind his back and handed them to Bev. "For you," he said. "As for my intentions, we're heading to dinner and a wreck room where we will take out our frustrations by smashing a room to smithereens."

Bev hummed. "The flowers are beautiful and the date sounds unique and lovely. Enjoy yourselves and be safe." She patted us both on the cheek before making her way toward the back of the house. She hadn't needed to stay to welcome my date—I figured it made her almost late for her new hobby of bingo with Eloise—but love washed over me to know that she'd wanted to be there for the milestone.

Cruz's eyes met mine and he reached for my hand before producing another bouquet of flowers. He leaned in and kissed my cheek. "Hi," he whispered gruffly. "You look fucking amazing."

"Looking pretty hot yourself." I smelled the flowers as my heart overflowed—they were another first for me. "Can we put these in water before we go?"

Cruz and I searched the kitchen before finding a vase under the sink. Once the flowers were trimmed and situated, I placed them on the counter. "I'll take them upstairs later. Thank you, I love them." Turning to face Cruz, I wrapped my arms around his neck. "No one has ever bought me flowers." I leaned in and pressed a kiss against his neck, savoring the scent and flavor of his skin.

Cruz's arms held me close, his hands caressing up and down my back. "I've never bought flowers for anyone. I'm glad it was you."

"Well, me and Bev," I teased.

Cruz laughed. "Figured a bit of bribery wouldn't hurt."

I stared up into Cruz's dark brown eyes. "I know it's our first date and all that, but since our order of events has been a bit messed up from the beginning, maybe I could kiss you now rather than waiting until after the date?"

He smiled and tugged me closer as he leaned into the corner of the counter and spread his legs so I could nestle between them. "As long as kissing after the date is a possibility."

Biting my lip, I hovered close to his mouth. "I think there's a very good possibility that we'll both be getting kisses tonight. Getting kisses, getting busy, getting lucky..." My last words were mumbled against his lips as I closed the space between us and captured his mouth.

Cruz groaned and the kiss quickly morphed from teasing and light to heavy and hot. We'd kissed and made out a lot since that first time and the heat and intensity never ebbed. Kissing Cruz always made me desperate and crazy, always wanting more.

As lips glided and teeth clicked, I pressed into Cruz and fought the urge to tell him we could skip the date and just go upstairs.

But he broke the kiss, both of us breathing heavily.

"Dinner with a boner should be fun," he teased as we rested our foreheads together. "Come on, let's go."

As we drove a couple towns over, Cruz took my hand. "I made reservations at a place I've never been, but now I'm realizing that I should have thought it through better because what if you don't like it or are allergic?"

I squeezed his hand. "Slow down." I ran a thumb over his knuckles. "I pretty much like all food and I don't know of any allergies, so unless it's someplace where we'll be asked to eat bugs or snakes or similar, it's probably fine."

Cruz let loose a whooshing breath. "I don't know why I'm so fucking nervous. You've become my best friend and we wake up in the same bed every damn day. A dinner date shouldn't be so hard."

"It's a first for both of us, makes sense we'd want to get it right." I leaned over and kissed his cheek. "If it turns out horrible, I'll still be in your bed tonight whether you like it or not."

He turned my way, deep brown eyes flashing with desire, with a smile. "Nowhere else I'd rather have you." Cruz returned his eyes to the road. "It's seafood, by the way. That okay?"

"I love seafood." I wrinkled my brow. "Well, I think I love seafood. I've never had super fresh or fancy stuff, but I like shrimp for sure. Should be fine."

Dinner ended up being the best food I'd ever eaten, but we both swore we'd never tell Bev. We each got a different meal and shared a variety of fish, shrimp, scallops, crab, lobster, and pasta. We skipped wine—some of the new medications I was on, thanks to Alicia and my new physician, maybe didn't mix so well with alcohol—but indulged in bread and salad along with our incredibly huge-portioned meal.

"You want dessert?" Cruz asked.

"Oh my God, it looks so delicious, but I don't know that I could possibly eat another bite."

"We could take it to go?" Cruz handed me the dessert menu.

We were already taking bread and part of our main dishes home, adding dessert seemed to make sense. "I guess we can eat it later." I bit my lip and studied the menu. "What are you getting?"

"Chocolate cake for sure. What about you?"

"I don't always love chocolate, but that lemon crème cake looks amazing."

We walked out of the restaurant a bit later and loaded our leftovers into the trunk.

"Our wreck time is in about forty-five minutes, but we're supposed to get there thirty minutes early to fill out forms and hear directions." Cruz pointed the car toward our destination. "There's a group option—which could be a lot of fun to bring the crew to—but I opted for it to be just us. Figured our first date and first time smashing a room together should be private."

"I'm excited, but also nervous, so I'm glad it's just us."

Later, after hearing the spiel and filling out the waiver forms, Cruz and I found ourselves dressed in ridiculous coveralls, gloves, and safety glasses that made us look like members of a scientific moving crew. Basically, the objective was to destroy the room. We were encouraged to break electronics, tear up furniture, smash walls, bust lamps, smash dishes, and whatever else we wanted to do in the tiny fake room.

Luckily, I had Cruz by my side because I wasn't sure I would have had the courage to throw the first plate. But Cruz rubbed his hands together and grinned as he walked to the shelving unit that held a stack of mismatched plates, bowls, and glasses.

"Let's do this." He picked up a plate and let it drop to the floor.

The resulting shattering noise made me jump, but I couldn't help a laugh that bubbled from deep within as I stared at the jagged pieces of the busted plate.

"Come on, your turn." Cruz handed me a plate.

I took it with shaking hands. I hadn't expected to be intimidated by the purpose of the place. But I realized quickly—probably thanks to all the talking I'd been doing with Alicia lately—that I'd spent over half of my life trying to keep myself alive, control whatever small bits I could, and hide from the bad— so letting go and purposely destroying the objects in the room kinda went against everything in me.

Strong arms wrapped around my waist and Cruz's warm breath whispered against my ear. "It's okay. I'm right here. We'll do it together." His hands closed around mine and we raised the plate to chest level. "On three, we throw it. One, two…" I shivered as his words washed over me. "…three."

Together, we tossed the plate to the ground and a sobbing laugh escaped my throat.

"You okay?" Cruz asked, his arms still holding me.

I nodded. "Yeah, can we do a few more?"

Cruz helped me through six more plates before I gathered the courage to venture to one of the lamps. I slammed it to the floor as a weird sort of warmth rolled through me. Unable to stop them, tears rolled down my face as I took a baseball bat to multiple televisions and computer monitors. Glasses, bowls, picture frames, I destroyed them all. By the time I took a sledge hammer to a kitchen chair and smashed a hole in the wall, I was screaming. When I finally stopped, letting the hammer fall from my hands as I stood in the middle of the obliterated room, my face wet with tears and throat raw from screaming, I glanced around. My head was in some sort of haze and I didn't completely remember the entire episode.

Cruz was beside me in a split second, holding me, rubbing my back, and just letting me catch my breath. When I finally pulled away from him, he lifted my chin and studied my face. "You okay?"

I nodded and looked around the room again. "Yeah. I wasn't expecting that—really don't know where it came from—but I think it was a good thing." Taking a shaky breath, I nuzzled into his neck. "But I'm so tired. Can we go home?"

Cruz kissed my temple. "Of course. Let's go."

I fell asleep on the way back to Remington Place and the next thing I knew, Cruz was tucking me into bed. "I'm sorry, I think I ruined our date," I mumbled.

"Never. I'm going to shower. Sleep."

"Need to shower, too."

"Sleep first, you're exhausted. You can shower when you wake." Cruz kissed the side of my head.

"Wanted a kiss. And we have leftovers to eat." I tucked my chin and didn't wake again until the bed dipped and I smelled food. I rolled over and checked the time. I wasn't sure the exact time Cruz had put me to bed, but I'd slept at least a few hours and it was past midnight. "You let me sleep so long."

"I crawled in and slept, too. You needed it." Cruz settled in next to me and pulled the tray to his lap. "But I woke up and needed to pee. Remembered the leftovers and thought they sounded good. So, I warmed the food up. You wanna eat?"

I shouldn't have actually been hungry, but I must have burned a lot of energy during my wrecking spree because I scarfed down my fair share of the leftovers.

"Oh my God, this cake is amazing." I moaned as I savored the lemon crème cake. "Here, taste it before you eat the chocolate. This is a light flavor and after chocolate it won't be the same."

I held my fork out and Cruz took the bite of cake. He closed his eyes as he chewed and nodded. "Yep, that's delicious. You want a bite of chocolate?"

I shook my head. "Nope, this is more than enough. I think I'm going to have a hard time going back to sleep, at least for a while."

"Go shower, then we can talk until we fall asleep."

Part of the reason we'd picked that night for a date was because neither of us had work early the next morning, so staying up way too late wasn't going to be a problem.

Making my way to the bathroom, I contemplated if I needed to do any preparations. Did I feel ready for sex with Cruz? Yes. Was I ready for full-on anal sex? Yes, but it was probably smarter to move a bit slower.

Alicia and I had been talking a lot about my limitations and expectations.

If she made me start thinking about or talking about the horrors of my past, I ran the gamut of anxiety, anger, crying, shutting down, and panic attacks.

If I thought about any type of sex with Cruz, I was fine. No issues.

Alicia suggested that was due to a combination of Cruz being my safe space and my brain being adept at pushing the past away and focusing only on the good with Cruz.

She had a lot to say about why it wasn't wise to continue just pushing the bad away, but so far, she hadn't had much luck getting me to wade into the horrors.

Climbing into the shower, I decided no anal prep aside from a thorough washing. I wanted Cruz and I to have sex, but no prep would assure I didn't let things move too far, too quickly.

You really think Cruz would let things move too quickly?

I laughed as I lathered my hair. No, Cruz would be hesitant to even do the things I was hoping for, he definitely wouldn't dive into anal sex just yet.

As I rinsed the shampoo from my hair and turned my attention to washing all the important crooks and crevices, a thought struck me. I wanted Cruz to fuck me someday, for sure. Would he ever want me to fuck him? At first examination of that thought, I hesitated. Would I be into that? Upon thinking further, I realized the thought of sliding my cock deep into Cruz—experiencing his tight heat and hearing the sounds he made as I fucked him—was not a turn-off.

If Cruz wanted me to top, I had no issue with it.

By the time I exited the shower, I was even more wide awake. I brushed my teeth and pulled on a pair of lounge pants before running the towel through my hair. I found Cruz in our dimly lit room, bare chested and scrolling his phone.

"Are you squinting? Is the text hard to read?" I teased as I hung up my wet towel. "We should look for reading glasses. Or, I think there's an elderly setting on your phone that can increase the size of the font to like eighty-seven or something."

Cruz dropped his phone on the bedside table with a laugh and patted the bed. "Come cuddle with me, you mouthy little shit. And I wasn't squinting. I was just interested in what I was reading. I have like seven to ten years before I should need reading glasses."

"If you say so. But if I notice it again or you start having headaches, I'm going to make an appointment with your eye doctor." I snuggled close to him. "It's part of my duty as the young person in the relationship. I have to care for my elderly person."

Cruz huffed and slapped a hand against my ass. "Better ways for you to take care of me." His words were gruff and suggestive and my belly fluttered with anticipation. "You wanna talk about what happened at the wreck room?"

I knew he wouldn't push me, but talking to Cruz was usually almost as helpful as talking to Alicia—sometimes even more. Taking a moment to gather my thoughts, I finally answered him. "I'll talk to Alicia about it, but I'm guessing—and I can only venture this guess because of things she and I have talked about during sessions—I finally let some of the fear and anger and pain from the past break through. I mean, it's not like those things aren't always with me." Cruz took my hand and kissed my knuckles. "But Alicia says—and I agree—that my brain has been in survival mode for so long—breaking things into categories and compartments—the way I think of it is like drawers I'm willing to open and drawers I keep locked up tight—and I naturally work to control what I allow in my head. Breaking those plates, smashing up that room, broke something loose in me. It's almost like everything I destroyed was a bad piece of my past and it got pretty emotional for me I guess."

"Do you feel better after doing it?" Cruz murmured into the top of my head, his nose nuzzling my damp hair.

"I do. I think if I'd gone in thinking it was a therapy exercise, I likely would have balked or held back. But being there with you and naturally letting go, it felt good. I wasn't expecting the way I responded to it, but it didn't feel like a bad thing." I ran my hand over Cruz's chest, smiling against his shoulder when his nipples formed pinkish-brown peaks.

"You're doing really well with Alicia," Cruz said.

I nodded. "I am. She's great. I'm learning to move on from things in the past and focus on the present and future with a more positive lens. It's not all fun and games; some of the stuff she wants me to talk about is just too hard right now. It's stuff that I can shut away, so I don't know why I need to talk about it." I teased my fingers in the furry black hair of Cruz's chest and abdomen.

"You'll get there. She knows what she's doing and you're the strongest person I know." Cruz ran his hand up and down my back. "You ever going to tell me about those nightmares? Maybe talking about them would help?"

I sighed. Part of the nightmares included horrors I had no desire to talk about with Alicia, let alone with Cruz. But he was so damn good to me, holding me through the terrorizing bad dreams and taking care of me while expecting nothing in return, I couldn't turn him down completely.

"Part of the nightmare always includes Lilly and Rusty. I was seventeen when Lilly brought Rusty to live with us. She had several other kids in other locations, but they were left to others for their care. Lilly was with me—and soon-to-be, Rusty—full time. I nearly puked when she brought him in. Thirteen, tiny, blond. I knew the moment I saw him that he'd had a rough time and Lilly would have her claws in him within days if she didn't already. I was the same age when she got to me and turned my life into a living hell. I'd been planning to leave—okay, you didn't just leave Lilly, I was planning to escape even if it killed me—but the moment I saw Rusty, I knew my plans needed to move more quickly.

"Lilly let Rusty go eat and play video games while she laughed about all the buyers who were excited to get dibs on him." I shuddered as the night came back to me. "She kept laughing and describing all these terrible things—things I'd lived through, but I couldn't think of them happening to that kid—and getting all handsy with me, telling me things she wanted to do to me." I paused and hoped my leftovers weren't going to make a comeback. "I shoved her away from me. She tripped over the kitchen rug and slammed her head against the counter before falling to the ground. There was so much blood and she never moved."

Cruz's arms tightened around me.

"I grabbed everything I had—I'd been slowly gathering bits and pieces for my eventual escape—and told Rusty we had to get out of there. I didn't want to scare the kid, but I gave him a Cliff Notes version of what Lilly was planning." I could still see the look of fear and confusion on Rusty's face. He'd wanted so badly to belong and be loved, but Lilly wasn't that person for him. "I dropped him at the foster agency. Knocked and made him promise he'd go in. No way I was going back there. I was nearly eighteen anyway. I waited in the shadows until someone came to the office door and let Rusty in."

We sat quietly for a while. I could almost feel questions pouring from Cruz, but he waited for me to go on.

"I assume I killed Lilly. It wasn't on purpose. But my nightmares usually involve some form of me being locked away because I killed her."

A rumbled sounded from Cruz's chest. "Fuck that. After what she did to you? No way."

"If she's dead—I don't know how she couldn't be, there was so much blood—there's no changing the fact that I killed her. On purpose or not, a person is dead and it's my fault." I shuddered. Yet another memory I'd been successful in locking away until it came to life in my nightmares.

"Have you told Alicia?"

I shook my head.

"Maybe you should? See what she suggests?"

"Tell my therapist I killed someone? That doesn't seem like a good move."

Cruz grunted. "Tell your therapist about the nightmares and that you fear you killed her, fear what could happen to you if you did." He kissed the top of my head. "She has rules she has to follow and unless the police are actively looking for you, she can't break confidentiality."

"Maybe. I'll think about it." Really, I'd pushed the memory of Lilly on the ground in a pool of blood so far from my mind that it hadn't crossed my mind to tell Alicia. I figured I'd just have to deal with the nightmares when they surfaced. "It's probably not a bad idea." I shifted so I could peer up at Cruz. "But can we shift gears a bit?"

Cruz nodded. "Tell me what you need."

I licked my lips. "I'm not ready for anal sex yet. And I can't do oral if you touch my head. Other than that, I don't think anything else will bother me." I rolled so I was on top of Cruz. "I want you so bad. Wanna touch and taste you."

Cruz groaned. "Want you, too. This is all in your control. You call the shots, you take what you need, you tell me what you want."

Cruz's words were equal parts empowering and intimidating. I'd never been in control of anything, let alone sex. Knowing that he was giving me all the power was heady stuff.

But it also scared the shit out of me. Who was I to call the shots? How could I be sure what I wanted? What if Cruz didn't like what I did?

He cupped my chin and brought my eyes to his and I realized I'd spaced out for a moment. "We can do as little or as much as you want. No pressure. What we've been doing so far has been more than enough. Your call; I will never push you for more than you're comfortable with."

I blushed, knowing he was referring to the heavy make-out sessions we'd been having. Who knew rubbing off against a guy while he kissed you and coming in your damn pants could be such a turn-on?

"Naked first. We'll go from there."

Cruz's eyes caught fire and his nostrils flared. "Naked sounds good. But we stop the moment you don't like something. No questions."

I nodded and rolled to my back to slide my pants off.

Cruz stood and slipped his own pants down his thick thighs, his heavy cock making my mouth water as he knee-crawled onto the bed. Kneeling next to me, he trailed a finger down my chest and abdomen, slowly tracing my V-line. "You're so fucking gorgeous."

My cock, not on board with the take it slow plan, bobbed against my belly. "Touch me." My words were needy, but I didn't care because I knew Cruz would never judge.

His big hand hovered just over my dick, close enough I could feel the warmth of his skin. When he finally made contact, I moaned and Cruz chuckled. "Shhh, we'll wake the whole house."

"Probably should kiss me to keep me quiet."

Cruz smiled and shifted so he could continue stroking me while devouring my mouth. For long moments, he kissed me and fisted my cock in slow, controlled strokes. Before breaking the kiss, he moved to tease my balls and run a finger over my hole.

Just when I was sure I'd blow my load at any moment, Cruz moved to lay on his back. "Straddle my chest and feed me that beautiful cock." He took my hand and squeezed. "If you're okay with it."

I scrambled to do what he said, liking that he made a decision even though the control was still mine. Settling my ass on his chest, loving the way my balls nestled against his warm skin, I smiled as Cruz licked his lips. "See something you like, old man?"

Cruz slapped my ass and I yelped.

"See this position in porn sometimes, never tried it." Cruz scoffed. "Hard to do something like this with a quickie in a bathroom stall. You good?"

I nodded. "Do you get a senior citizen discount on your porn? Can we share accounts to save money?"

He gripped my ass and squeezed. "I'm thinking maybe we should switch positions. Shoving a dick in your mouth may be the only way to shut you up."

I laughed. "No reason to waste this opportunity." I took my hard length in hand and smeared the leaking head against Cruz's lips. "Open up."

His tongue flicked out to lick my head before parting his lips and taking each inch of my long cock as I fed it to him. The wet heat of Cruz's mouth and his fiery eyes that never left mine were enough to send me over the edge, but I squeezed my base and pulled out. Breathing hard, I chuckled. "Okay, this will be over in a nanosecond if I don't get a grip. I don't want to come too soon; I have other things I want to do."

"We've got all the time in the world," Cruz assured as he stroked up and down my back. "There's no hurry, no race, no schedule and checklist of what we have to do and when. Knowing you're so close just from my mouth is fucking sexy as hell. So what if you shoot now? There's always later. Plus, you're young, we can find out what your rebound time is like."

God, I loved this man.

Shit. The thought ricocheted around my head. Did I love Cruz? Yeah, I did. But now was not the time to be thinking about it and definitely not the time to be saying it out loud.

I returned to the task at hand and slid my cock back between Cruz's lips. Taking hold of the headboard, I rocked my hips and gazed in wonder as my cock slipped in and out of his mouth. Shiny wet with his saliva and rock hard, my dick throbbed and my balls drew up tight. Increasing my speed, I groaned when Cruz gripped my ass, spreading my cheeks to tease a finger against my hole. That was all it took before I threw my head back and moaned as an orgasm washed over me, my release coating Cruz's tongue.

He continued to play with my hole and tongue

my cock until it was too much and I had to pull away. Watching him lick his lips as drops of my cum dribbled down his chin was something I'd never tire of.

"Want to suck you," I said.

"No hands on your head, right?"

I nodded. Unsure if I'd ever work through that limitation, I wasn't anywhere close to being able to try it at that point.

"No worries. What if you turn around? You can suck me and I'll be busy eating your ass and not even able to reach your head." Cruz cocked his head and waited as I thought about the proposed position.

I maneuvered myself on Cruz's chest and reached for his thick cock. Hard and heavy, his length filled my hand. "Don't know how this will ever fit, but I'm totally looking forward to the challenge."

Cruz chuckled. "You okay with rimming?"

I swallowed thickly and glanced over my shoulder. "Yeah. I'll stop you if it's too much." I bent at the waist and nuzzled my nose against Cruz's belly, the thatch of dark hair, and finally the silky skin of his shaft. As I swirled my tongue around his head, Cruz spread my ass and pressed his lips against my most sensitive skin. I gasped, dropping my head to his hip. "Shit, I don't know if I can suck cock while getting rimmed."

With a swipe of his tongue from my balls to my hole, Cruz reached to stroke my already reawakening dick. "You're talented, I bet you can. But only do what feels right."

Cruz's hot cock rested against my cheek while I tried to gather myself—which was a great feat with a tongue swirling around my hole.

I shifted and took Cruz's length in hand before parting my lips and sliding my mouth down his shaft. Using my hand to keep him from going too deep, I found a slick, wet rhythm as I bobbed up and down. With his tongue on my hole while he played with my balls and stroked my now hard dick, I moaned around him when I realized I'd definitely be blowing my load again.

For long moments, the only sounds that filled the room were the sloppy wet noises of mouths, lips, and tongues against hot skin. When my balls drew up tight, I whimpered, disappointed that it would be over soon, but longing for the release.

"Is a finger okay?" Cruz's gruff words broke through my cock-sucking haze.

"Oh, God, yes," I begged. I wanted everything with this man. Every touch, every moment with him took me away from my past and gave me hope for the future.

I continued to suck him, loving that he knew not

to thrust hard or deep. Moving to cup his balls and finding them drawn and tight, I reveled in the knowledge that he was close and I had brought him to that point.

A warm, wet finger pressed against my entrance and I tensed for a brief moment.

"Okay? We can stop, you tell me." Cruz rubbed his finger in slow, gentle circles on my puckered skin.

"I'm good. Wanna feel it." I pushed my ass toward him as I took him back in my mouth.

Cruz worked his finger in slowly, the biting stretch stinging only briefly, and I moaned around his shaft.

"Oh fuck," Cruz panted. "That's so fucking good. Love your mouth on my cock." He pulled his finger out, chuckling as I whimpered, and added more spit to my already soaked hole. The digit slipped in easier that time and my balls tingled.

"Do two," I said.

Cruz complied, adding a second finger and I shamelessly pushed my ass into his touch. "Oh, fucking shit, that's good." Returning most of my focus to Cruz's cock, I sucked and stroked, loving the salty flavor of his pre-cum on my tongue. I wanted more.

"Lo, baby, I'm close. Pull off if you need to."

Cruz's warning came at the exact moment his fingers made contact with the bundle of nerves deep inside and I lost it.

As Cruz's cock pulsed his release in my mouth, my own orgasm spilled hot and slick between our bodies. Between rutting my throbbing shaft against his chest, my ass clenching around his fingers, and Cruz's flavor exploding in my mouth, I wasn't sure I'd ever come down from the high.

When we finally broke our connection and took a moment to clean up, I was hit with a warm, cozy feeling—like everything in my life was right. I crawled into bed and let Cruz wrap me in his arms.

I love you. The words were right there, clawing their way up my throat, but I swallowed them down. It was too soon, I had too much to work through. Would a declaration of love scare Cruz away?

"That was fucking amazing," Cruz whispered against my head. "You are amazing."

"Thank you for being patient with me. There's no one else I'd rather have these firsts with than you." I yawned. "You wore me out."

"Not bad for an old man, huh?"

I smiled against his chest. "Just remember, we're at two to one, my lead. Think you can go again?"

Cruz snorted. "Right now? Hell, no." His arm tightened around me. "After we sleep? Bring it on."

We were quiet for several moments before Cruz spoke again.

"Have you ever thought about topping?"

I didn't even open my heavy eyes, just sighed into him. "Not until you. But now? If it was something you wanted? Definitely."

His hand traveled down my arm until he found my hand. Lacing our fingers together, he gave me a squeeze. "Good to know because I'm very interested."

With a flutter of anticipation in my chest, I caressed his thumb with mine as sleep carried me away.

We woke a few hours later just as the first rays of sunlight were lighting up the dark sky. Knowing neither of us needed to get up early, I smiled sleepily as I thought of wake-up sex and a few more hours of sleep.

Cruz shifted behind me, his morning erection nudging my ass.

"Good morning." I took hold of his hand and guided it to my hard, naked cock. "Looks like we've both got a problem. Any idea how we can take care of it?"

He chuckled. "I've got some ideas." Cruz rolled me to my back and settled himself between my legs, our hard lengths rubbing together. "This okay?"

"Sooo, okay." I pulled him down for a kiss, hoping our shared morning breath would cancel each other out, and moaned when his tongue glided against mine.

Cruz lifted up on his arms, breaking the kiss so he could watch our bodies as we rocked our hips and rutted together. "So fucking gorgeous," he murmured before capturing my mouth again as he thrust hard and slow against me.

When he had me writhing and panting, he took both of our cocks in his big hand and began to stroke. Swiping his thumb over our slits, smearing the pre-cum, he jacked us as he kissed my neck and whispered sexy praise in my ear.

My moans and whimpers increased until Cruz crushed his mouth to mine to keep me quiet. I shuddered as my cock erupted, hot cum pouring over Cruz's fist. He drew away from my mouth and glanced between us to watch, his own release following quickly after mine as our cum flowed together, coating his hand and my belly.

We kissed for a long moment before Cruz declared he was sticky. He grabbed a towel and wiped us up the best he could before pulling on shorts and making a dash to the bathroom. When he returned with two wet cloths, my heart clenched at the way he always took care of me.

After we cleaned up, I slid into some shorts and set an alarm. "We've got like four hours to sleep."

"Perfect. Come here." Cruz yanked me onto the bed and tucked me into his chest before pulling the covers up to our shoulders.

"Thank you for the best first date ever," I whispered. "You've ruined me for all others."

Cruz kissed the top of my head. "You're welcome. We'll need to plan a second after your surgery."

There was a lot of fixes and healing ahead of me, but I felt strong with Cruz by my side.

NINE
CRUZ

"You look beat. How was your time with Alicia?" I flopped on the couch next to Logan where he was curled up absently staring at an afternoon movie on the TV.

"Glad I took today off, I'm worn out. Tomorrow at three different shifts will be a bitch, but I'm mostly feeling better." He sat up and shifted to my arms.

His surgery had gone well. Logan had requested that I be the one the doctor spoke to after the procedure and I sat with him in recovery while his groggy, loopy ass woke up. He'd been adorable as the drugs wore off, but I hated that this throat hurt so much.

The doctor had declared that Logan's tonsils were

terribly scarred and his ears were some of the worst he'd ever seen. The tube placement had taken longer than usual due to all the gunk he had to clear away. But the tubes were now in place and his tonsils and adenoids were gone; the doctor suspected Logan would be a lot healthier from that point on.

I'd spent as much of Saturday and Sunday with him as possible, leaving him in Bev's capable hands when I had to work. She kept him supplied with warm soothing soups and icy cold slushies.

By Sunday, Logan was feeling better. Still tired and his throat was sore, but he declared it was nothing like when he was sick so it was bearable. Plus, he was so amazed at how much better he could hear, he counted the whole thing as a good decision and huge success.

His doctor had suggested he take Monday off and said he'd write an excuse from work for up to a week if needed. Of course, Logan had balked at that. He loved working—both from the income aspect and because he simply enjoyed his jobs and the people he worked with. He'd agreed to the one day off, but had refused to cancel his appointment with Alicia.

"Alicia was good. I told her about the wreck room."

I nuzzled the top of his head and kissed his

temple. Watching him zone out and destroy that room and then break down crying had been scary. Part of me figured it was good for him to get those emotions out, but I worried about pushing too far. "What did she say?"

"Pretty much what I'd already figured. Lots of repressed emotions, a whole shit ton of things I haven't allowed myself to think about." He shrugged against me. "She said the wreck room isn't unlike some of the exercises she has clients do, but it's just set up as fun rather than therapy. I guess breaking things kinda knocked something loose inside and it all came out."

"We can go again, if you want. Maybe take the whole group?"

Logan drew in a deep breath. "Maybe. It's not like that one time cured me of anything. Alicia says it's a good exercise, but I need to include talking about the past." He shuddered. "I don't get why she's so dead set on me talking about that nightmare. It's done, over, I just want to move on."

I wasn't sure I could handle hearing specific details about the horrors he lived through, but I could see the benefit of talking about them. "I get that." It wasn't my place to push. Alicia knew what she was doing and would eventually get him there; I'd be there to support him.

"I told her about Lilly."

"Yeah?"

"I mean, I'd told her about Lilly before. But this time I told her about what happened when I pushed her."

I held him tighter. I didn't care if that piece of shit was dead, but I couldn't lie and say I wasn't slightly terrified of what might happen if Logan's push had killed her. He'd been seventeen, it was over three years ago, she was a sexual predator, and it was in self-defense. Still, if she was dead, would any of that matter? Would Logan be taken from me? "What did she say?"

"She wanted to know if I'd ever looked her up online or tried to find out what happened to her."

"And?"

"Hell, no. I can barely stomach saying that monster's name let alone purposely looking for her." Logan ran his hand up and down my arm. "She said she'd look into it and see what she could find out. I guess you were right about the confidentiality shit and all that. Unless police come looking for me and asking her questions in an official murder case, she can't tell anyone what I told her." He was quiet for a moment, but I knew him well enough now to know he had more to say. "I'm so screwed up over it. Part of me wants her to be alive so there's no chance of me being responsible for her murder. But part of me hopes that bitch died in a pool of her own blood. Like long days of agony, a slow, painful death. And then I realize how fucked up my head is."

I squeezed him tightly against me. "No. I think those feelings are very normal and I can definitely see both sides of what you're saying. Let Alicia look into it. Let her help you work through the past. You're moving on because you're strong and good and deserve so much, but maybe letting her help with the past would take away the weight of it hanging over your head?"

"Yeah, maybe. It's just that things are going so well and it scares me to think about unpacking all of it."

"It's your call. I'll be here either way."

"Thank you," Logan whispered. "I think I need a nap before dinner."

"Well, I need a shower first. How about you go curl up in bed and I'll nap with you once I'm cleaned up. We've got a couple hours before dinner." I stood and pulled him to his feet.

Later, after chatting with some of my housemates and taking a shower, I entered our room quietly. Padding softly to the bed, I couldn't help the catch in my chest when I looked down at Logan's beautiful face as he slept.

I'd never been in love. Was what I felt for Logan love? Wasn't it too quick? Too much, too soon, right? Would it freak Logan out if he knew how I felt about him?

Crawling into bed and wrapping Logan in my arms, I decided there was no need to rush it. If I loved him, I loved him and that wouldn't change. Logan had a lot to work through, so I wasn't going to throw in those three words that could potentially cause him a problem. Falling in love with a guy fifteen years younger than me had never been a goal, but the moment Logan entered my life it was like I was set on a path I had no control over. I guess love doesn't care what your plans are, love happens whether you're expecting it or not.

I kissed the top of his head and settled in. Naps were always great; naps with Logan in my arms were absolutely perfect.

"EVERYONE GRAB chairs from the shop while I get the fire going." Jesse was busy building a pile of wood in the firepit. "Fridge is stocked, get what you want."

"I'll get the food," Cooper announced. "Bev sent over some dips and appetizers."

The whole crew, sans Hadley and Bev, had taken an outing to the first home football game of the season. Logan had gotten teary-eyed when I'd asked if it was something he wanted to do, and I think he'd had a good time.

The game itself had been an absolute blow-out, but the group had laughed and joked, cheered, walked the grounds, and done some people watching. By the end of the third quarter, we'd opted to take our little party back to Jesse's for food, drinks, and a fire.

One thing I'd learned about living in a Midwestern town like Remington is that a fire with food and drinks was always a draw. I'd been shocked to learn that both Dre and Khi had agreed to come to the game and the after party. Having the whole group together was nice.

We gathered our chairs in a circle around the fire pit and I moved to help Cooper set up a table with chips, dips, wings, sliders, meatballs, and bacon-wrapped sausages. Damn, I'd told Bev we were going to the game and having a little gathering after and she'd offered to make a few snacks.

"I think Bev's idea of a few snacks is a lot different than mine," I told Cooper as we opened bags of chips and put spoons in dips. "I would have had a bag of pretzels and some chips and salsa at most."

Cooper laughed. "Bev is too good to us, but she also adores cooking. The moment you mentioned this, she was tutting around chattering away about the menu she wanted to make."

"I feel bad she made all of this and isn't even here."

"Nah, she and Hadley were going to have a very special tea-party-style dinner, bake some cookies, and watch a movie before heading to bed. They're probably both conked out as we speak." Cooper put a stack of plates and a handful of plastic forks on the table. "She doesn't enjoy late nights. We can make it up to her by being at Thursday dinner and talking up how delish these snacks are."

Over the next few minutes, everyone mingled, filled their plates, and sat down around the fire to stuff our faces. The food was seriously amazing, but more than that, the camaraderie went straight to my heart.

But the true treat was getting to watch the night through Logan's eyes. Sometimes it was easy to forget the enormous amount of normal teen experiences Logan missed out on.

He'd been shocked to see how full the parking lot had been when we arrived for the game. "This many people want to watch high school football?" he'd mused.

"It's almost a religion in these parts, second only to basketball," Dalton had told him.

Once the food was covered, everyone grabbed more water, pop, and beer before getting comfy by the fire. The warm orange glow that washed over all of us was beautifully heartwarming, and when Logan took my hand and squeezed, I knew the setting— gathered with friends—was having an effect on him as well.

"So, what did you think of your first high school sporting event?" Jesse asked.

Logan smiled. "It was amazing. The cheerleaders were good, but seemed a bit plastic. The football game itself confused me, but the uniform pants get an A+ in my book."

"Here, here," I tapped my bottle against Logan's soda can.

"The band and dance team were fantastic, I'd go again just to watch them perform," Logan said. "I think the biggest thing that shocked me was all the different groups of people."

"What do you mean?" Cooper asked.

"Well, I was never in one place long enough to fit in with any one group, but I definitely noticed the different cliques or whatever they're called. I just never realized how many of the different groups would come hang out at a football game. Some of them, I get, but some of the people there seemed all sorts of out of place." Logan shrugged. "I expected to see the popular people—the jocks, the cheerleaders, that type—but I think I saw kids from almost every single type of crowd. Granted, most were all congregated together, but I just never really thought I'd see nerds, grunge, goth, and theater kids at football."

Rai laughed. "As a proud high school nerd, I can assure you that they were there solely for socializing within their crew. We used to go to all the games and think we were the total shit. I'm sure some of the groups go to make fun of others, some go to be ironic, and some go to actually watch the game. The band kids have to be there, but I bet they'd go even if it wasn't a requirement." He and Spencer had their chairs pressed together and Rai cuddled under Spencer's arm.

"I never really got to figure out where I would have fit in," Logan said absently and he seemed to space out for a bit. "What groups were all of you in during high school?"

"Nerd, high achiever, gamer," Rai offered.

Spencer kissed the top of his head. "Pissed-off loaner and reluctant jock."

Dalton glanced at Gabby and she shrugged. "I was popular, but only within a subset of the high school. Like middle-of-the-road popular. But I got good grades and was friendly with almost everyone. Teachers liked me."

Dalton smiled. "Of course they did, what's not to like? I was good in school, played some sports, didn't really have one single group to hang with. I was kinda on the periphery of several. Just wanted to have fun, get good grades, and move on to college."

The sharing seemed to be moving in a circle and it was Jesse's turn.

"Did they even have high school when you were young?" Cooper batted his lashes innocently and Jesse shot him a look. "Did you have to walk to school, uphill both ways and use your slate board? Ohhhh, did you tie a belt around your books to carry them?"

"Are you done?" Jesse deadpanned.

Cooper nodded his head with an angelic smile.

"I was friendly with a lot of people, Robby being my best friend of course. But I was also working hard to keep myself as deep in the closet as possible, so I'm not sure I enjoyed high school as much as I possibly could have." Jesse shrugged. "It was fun and I had great friends—I don't regret ending up with Nicole because that led to Lauren and Hadley—just sometimes wonder what it would have been like to know myself better back then." He turned toward Cooper. "While I don't even like to think of you in high school—because it reminds me just how damn old I am—your turn."

Cooper placed his hand on Jesse's thigh. Jesse covered Cooper's hand with his own. "Well, I was a total spaz. Better than elementary school, but so much worse than now. I'd figured out some coping skills for ADHD and dyscalculia, but they maybe weren't the healthiest and I didn't like myself much. If you can believe it, I was a lot snarkier and unfiltered back then than I am now. Most people didn't appreciate it."

Chuckles filled the circle as we all thought of what Cooper would have been like as a kid.

The circle of eyes turned to me. "I spent most of my high school years just trying to blend in, figure out a way to fit without giving up part of myself or calling attention to what made me different. I went to a small, strict Catholic school. I was one of the only brown-skinned kids there. No one really bothered me for my Mexican heritage, but it was kinda insinuated that I didn't need to flash it around. That's why I always appreciated my parents allowing me to learn about where I came from. I knew I was gay but scared to death to add one more thing to the list of differences. Plus, my parents didn't have a lot of money so that was one more thing that set me apart. Mostly, I did well in classes, did my best to hide the real me while struggling to stay out of trouble and blend in with the entire school. It was exhausting."

"Did your parents tell you about your birth mother?" Gabby asked.

I smiled. "Yeah, I have a few pictures stowed away. She was only fifteen when she got pregnant with me. No clue who my bio father is, supposedly she refused to tell for fear of getting him in trouble. I like to think maybe they were just young and stupid in love. She went to live with the nuns until I was born. Her name was Maria Cruz; that's where Mom and Dad got my name."

"Have you ever looked for her?" Logan asked as he stroked my hand.

I shook my head. "Nah, do you know how many Maria Cruz names there are in the world? Things worked out the way they were supposed to and I was blessed with my parents."

Khi cleared his throat. "Do you all really think that? When you talk about things working out the way they're supposed to, you're serious?" His question was less confrontational and more just pained curiosity.

I nodded. "I do. If my parents hadn't adopted me, who knows what kind of life I would have had with a fifteen-year-old unwed mother in Mexico. I mean, I still have major regrets over prison—sometimes wish I could go back and stop myself from hanging with that particular group of guys on that particular night —but I learned a lot about myself during those years and I try to focus on the good rather than the bad and things I can't change. Biggest wish is that I could have had more time with my parents; I'll never believe that my incarceration wasn't a huge factor in their deaths."

Logan squeezed my hand.

Khi glanced around the circle as if waiting for more people to speak.

"I'm not yet at a point where I can say I think things worked out for the best." Logan's voice was small and haunted. "I'm working through a lot of things. Don't know that I'll ever be able to see my past as something positive—and I think that's okay. But I do know that being in the alley behind the Wishing Well that night was a fate type thing that seems to be working out very well." He leaned over and pressed a kiss to my cheek.

Spencer cleared his throat. "Along the same lines as Logan, I can't say that I appreciate the shit in my past—it messed me up pretty bad—but I can say that

I definitely ended up right where I want to be. I can't change my past, but I can focus on the good in my present and future."

Khi looked at Jesse.

"I get what you're asking and I've had the same thoughts so many times. Can I really be glad my wife and daughter died just because it forced me to be Hadley's dad and brought me to Cooper?" Jesse shook his head. "I've worked through this a lot with Alicia. I'll never be grateful Nicole and Lauren died. I'll always wonder what would have happened between Nicole and me—we were separating and planning on counseling. I'd like to think we would have parted as close to amicably as possible. Would I have moved to Remington after that? Left Lauren and Hadley behind only to visit them from time-to-time? I really don't know." Jesse wrapped his arm around Cooper. "But the thing is, I can't change the past. What happened to Nicole and Lauren was a terrible accident and I wish with every fiber of my being that it didn't happen. But it did. And I moved on—eventually. Moving on brought me to Remington where I found my place, found my family." He leaned over and kissed the side of Cooper's head. "Found my forever. So, do I think things turned out the way they were supposed to? Yes. Do I like the way I got here? Not so much.

Would I change things? I've started not playing that game because it was making me insane. I can't change what happened, so there's no reason to even entertain the question."

The circle was quiet for a while until Logan cleared his throat. "What about you, Khi? What were you like in high school?"

Khi frowned and shot a glance at Dre. "Poor family, wrong side of the tracks, constantly having to prove myself. I was good at sports which was my only saving grace. Grades were good enough to stay on the team at least. Sports were the only thing that kept me from being an outcast."

Dre shifted and studied Khi. "That's not how I would have described you at all."

Khi shot daggers at Dre. "Yeah, well, you were in ninth grade, I was in twelfth, it's not like we saw that much of each other."

Dre studied Khi as if remembering something, but said nothing.

"Were you out in high school?" Logan asked. Khi had talked just enough about himself in the time he'd been at Remington Place to know he was gay and coming out of a bad breakup.

"Yeah," Khi answered with a nod. "I wasn't throwing rainbow parades or tossing glitter bombs, but those closest to me knew and I didn't deny it.

Earning sports scholarships was my main focus so I didn't worry too much about anything else. But I refused to hide who I was. People already looked down on my family because we were poor, might as well give them plenty to judge." He threw a glance toward Dre. "Lying to yourself and others just to protect your perfect life is a shit way to live." Khi leaned back in his chair and seemed ready to stop talking about himself.

"Well, I guess that leaves me." Dre blinked as if surfacing from a memory. "I was a band geek in middle school and came to high school ready to grow that status. I also loved all things theater and spent a lot of time creating costumes. I made good grades because anything less was not accepted in my house. I had a few close friends, but for the most part, I didn't feel like I fit in. High school wasn't bad for me, but I definitely didn't know myself well enough back then. Kinda wish I could go back and change things."

"What would you change?" Cooper asked.

Dre shrugged. "I was Narnia-deep in the closet— like to the point where I was actually looking at conversion camps and trying to figure out a way to get my parents to pay for it without letting them know I was gay—at the time I didn't know the word pansexual." He ignored Khi's huff of disgust. "I was so afraid of anyone finding out I was queer that I spent a lot of energy judging and deriding the openly queer kids." He shook his head. "I wasn't a bully, but I made it clear I didn't approve of their choices—most of which I learned from my parents." Dre shrugged. "I know myself a lot better now. I have regrets from high school, but I can't change them now, so I just want to be the best me and move forward."

Khi snorted and stood. "It's been fun, but I'm out. Later."

We all stared at Khi's back as he walked through the gate and toward Bev's place.

"What was that?" Spencer asked.

Gabby glanced at Dre before shrugging. "Khi and Dre go way back and they're not happy memories. Dre and I were freshmen when Khi was a senior. Dre and I were in the band, choral, theater, and dance departments a lot so we knew each other a bit. I'm not privy to their rift, but there's been no love lost between them."

Dre gathered his braids and tied them back with a band. "We've always rubbed each other the wrong way—we're still very different, but we were even more so in high school. His hatred for me seems a lot worse now. I'm guessing the breakup didn't help his disposition."

I got the feeling there was more to Dre and Khi's history, but wasn't going to pry.

"The breakup was bad. And he's not always so grumpy." Gabby defended her brother. "He just seems extra abrasive around you."

The group eventually broke up and helped gather trash, fold up chairs, and put food away before saying good night and making our way home.

By the time Logan and I reached our room, I wondered if he'd be ready to just crash, but the way he wrapped his arms around my neck and kissed me told me otherwise.

"You have thirty minutes to shower and meet me back here. I'm going to see if the downstairs bathroom is open," he murmured against my neck. "If you were serious about bottoming, take a few extra minutes. No pressure, just wanted you to know I'm on board."

We broke apart, my cock already throbbing and my heart thumping against my chest. "I'll see you in thirty minutes," I said against Logan's lips before swatting at his ass as he hurried down the stairs.

When I returned, Logan was stretched out on the bed in our dimly lit room.

"You're late," he accused with a smirk.

"I had things to do." I winked and snapped the towel in his direction.

He bit his lip. "You're forgiven."

Letting the towel fall to the floor, I crawled onto the bed and gathered Logan in my arms. As he rolled me to my back and kissed me, I couldn't help but worry.

"You okay?" Concern etched Logan's brow. "It's okay if you don't want to do this with me. I know it's probably hard to get over my past." He swallowed thickly as tears shone in his eyes and he dipped his head.

"Hey." I cupped his chin and gently lifted his face until his eyes met mine. "My nerves have nothing to do with not wanting to do this with you. I want anything and everything you feel comfortable giving me." I ran a thumb over his bottom lip. "I nearly busted a nut in the shower just thinking about you fucking me."

Logan's eyes searched mine as if trying to determine if my words were true. "Then what's the problem?"

I stroked my hands up and down Logan's back, loving the way his slim waist flared at the hips and led to that gorgeously round, fleshy ass. "I'm scared that something we do together will bring up bad memories. I don't want anything we do to hurt you in any way."

Logan cocked his head and smiled softly before

rolling from on top of me and settling in at my side. "You're probably the sweetest man on the face of this earth. I get what you're saying and I appreciate you thinking about me." His hand caressed over my chest, lightly toying with a nipple as I willed my cock to behave when we'd clearly paused and moved to having a serious conversation. "This is something I've talked about with Alicia. I don't know why, but the bad shit never haunts me when I'm with you. Your kisses and touches never bring back the past. Nothing we've ever done scares me or makes me sink into that darkness."

"I love knowing that and I feel privileged to be that person for you," I swallowed thickly, "but what if it's just not happened yet? What if we take a next step and something clicks and makes the past come barreling back?"

"That's kinda what I live with on a daily basis." Logan shrugged. After a moment, he took a deep breath. "It's why Alicia is so adamant that I talk about the past. She says that if I can talk about it, give voice to my fear and pain, it will go a long way in taking away the power my past has on me." He shook his head. "Not that it will ever go away completely, but she says voicing it and letting it out is a good first step in taking back the power and letting go of the darkness."

"That makes a lot of sense. How do you feel about it?"

"I agree that it makes sense. There's a part of my head," he tapped at his temple, "that realizes Alicia is right." He pressed his lips together. "But another part is terrified of opening that box of horrors because if they start to get out, I may never get them back in again." He shuddered. "I just don't know that I can survive letting it all out."

"Do you trust Alicia?"

Logan nodded. "I do." He frowned. "She says you're my safe space, but she's also warned that, as I start working through the past, I may have some setbacks in all areas of my life—including sex." He worried his bottom lip.

"If you're brave enough and strong enough to work with Alicia the way she's requesting, then you and I can work through whatever bumps in the road you may have." I leaned closer and kissed his nose. "If that means changing things up, fine. If it means a complete halt, don't worry about it. We'll figure it out. The main thing is healing you."

Logan huffed. "That means so much to me, but I want to argue that we could avoid any setbacks and issues if Alicia would just let me ignore the past and move on."

I thought about that for a second. "I don't think

she'd ever force you to delve into that part of your life, do you?"

He shook his head. "No. She wouldn't. I know that. She's said it has to be my decision. If I take the step, she'll be there to help me work through it."

I pulled him close and kissed the top of his head. "I will, too. I know I'm not a professional, but I want to help in whatever way I can."

"You've already done so much for me. So much I don't deserve and can never pay back." Logan pressed his head against my chest.

"You deserve the world—and I'd mean that even if I wasn't falling head-over-heels in love with you." I froze. Well, shit. I hadn't meant to spill that tidbit at that exact moment. "And you never owe me anything," I finished lamely, my eyes studying Logan to see if he'd caught what I'd said and was freaking out.

Logan's bright eyes stared up at me and he chewed on his bottom lip. "You're falling for me?"

Of course, he'd heard that part loud and clear. I took a deep breath. "Yeah. Sorry, I didn't mean to blurt that out. I know you've got more than enough to deal with right now."

He shook his head and smiled. "No, it's perfect. I've been so worried about how you'd feel if you knew I was falling in love with you. Knowing we both feel the same makes it easier."

The vice grip on my heart loosened and I breathed a bit easier. "I've never been in love before," I brushed my lips over his.

"Me neither. Another first we can share." Logan pulled back. "Um, Alicia has mentioned that I could have you come to appointments if I wanted."

I cocked a brow. "Do you want?"

He shrugged. "I don't know. You already do so much for me, plus, you have work and everything. Not to mention, it's kinda embarrassing to bring your boyfriend to your therapy appointments—I don't exactly need you figuring out just how fucked up I am."

My heart did an impersonation of a hummingbird trying to flap out of my chest. "Boyfriend?" My words were gravely and my chest ached with how badly I longed for him to say yes.

Logan's cheeks pinked and he dipped his head. "Well, we sleep in the same bed, went on a date, we're having sex, and just admitted we're falling in love...boyfriend kinda seemed like a no-brainer. But if you're not okay with that..."

I gripped the back of his neck and pulled him in for a searing kiss, groaning into his mouth as he whimpered and stroked my tongue with his. When we broke apart, I pressed my forehead against his and caught my breath. "Boyfriend is perfect." I smacked a kiss against his lips. "You are perfect." Another kiss. "I have the perfect boyfriend."

Logan giggled and kissed me, long and slow. "I love you, Cruz," his raspy whisper was so very soft, but I heard it all the way to my core.

"I love you. And I will attend every single appointment you need me to. Boyfriend or not—never think I'm only with you because of sex or dating or whatever. I'm your friend and I want to be there for you whether we're romantically involved or not." I got the feeling that Logan often felt he needed to use sex and similar as payment and I never wanted him to think he owed me.

"I'll talk to Alicia. Maybe. I just don't want to add one more thing to your plate that has to do with me; you've already done so much."

"I wouldn't do it if I didn't care," I assured him. I shifted and pulled him on top of me. "Now, if you're still interested, I believe we were on the brink of you introducing my ass to your cock."

A laugh bubbled from Logan. "Were we? I don't recall." He cocked his head and pursed his lips.

I slapped a hand on his perfect bubble butt. "I want you inside me." With my hands on his ass, I thrust my hips up so our quickly-hardening cocks could rub together. "Please."

Logan groaned and dropped his mouth to mine. "I've never…"

"Me neither. We'll figure it out together."

"Lube? Condoms?" Logan pushed up on his arms so he could look down at me.

I rolled him to his back, my body coming to rest on top of him as I reached under the bed and yanked out a plastic bag. I found the bottle of lube and condoms I'd purchased recently. "We're set." I tossed them to the mattress and rolled over again so Logan was on top of me.

"How do you want to do this?" Logan asked with a tremor in his voice.

"Whatever feels right for you. I don't care if all we do is kiss and frot until we both get off. Blow jobs? Rimming? It's all good, I promise."

"But you'd be okay with me fucking you?" Logan rolled his hips, his hard cock rutting against mine.

I closed my eyes and moaned. "So. Very. Okay."

"That's what I want."

"I'm yours, do whatever you want."

Logan shifted and shoved a pillow under my ass before settling between my thighs, my legs over his shoulders.

With long slim fingers, he parted my ass cheeks

and licked a swipe from cleft to taint and back again before honing in on my hole.

"Fuck, Lo. Oh fuck, that's good."

He continued to swirl his tongue against my pucker as my heavy cock leaked onto my stomach. Logan pressed his tongue into me, working at the tight ring of muscle as I groaned and gripped the sheets.

"You want my finger?" Logan asked.

"Want your dick," I groused.

He chuckled. "Patience, old man. At your age, it's important to go slow. Don't want to push your luck."

I growled and struggled into a sitting position so I could pull Logan into my arms and devour his mouth. Savoring the flavor of myself on his tongue, I thrust and swirled my tongue in his mouth the way he'd done in my ass.

He pulled back with a smile and fiery eyes. "You want my finger or not?"

I grunted and flopped back down as Logan used the lube to slick his digit and my ass. "Tell me if I need to stop."

I knew one finger wasn't going to be a problem. With as slender as Logan's hands were, three fingers would probably be needed to open me up enough. That didn't stop my gasp when his slick finger breached my ring. The sting was brief and I immediately wanted more. "Add another. Fuck, Lo, so good."

"You're so damn hot and tight," Logan marveled, "I'll bust a nut the moment I'm inside." He added a second finger and slid deep until the tips brushed against my bundle of nerves and I nearly came off the bed. Logan grinned up at me. "Prostate?"

"Prostate," I agreed, breathless and dying for more.

"Think you can take a third? I'm not huge, but I don't want to hurt you."

I nodded. "Make it quick, I need that dick." I'd been turned into a begging, rhyming, gooey pile of desire and I didn't even care.

Logan took a few moments to stretch me, pausing briefly when the stretch was almost too much for me, and then reached for the condom and more lube. "Wanna watch you come first or come together. Not sure it's possible, but that's the goal."

I pulled my knees back, opening my ass for him. "If not, you can suck me off after or I'll jerk off and paint your face. Either way, we're both getting off."

Logan took his place between my legs and pressed the head of his cock against my entrance. I groaned as his length slid into me inch-by-inch, stretching my tight hole. What Logan lacked in girth, he more than made up for in length and a perfect curve—a fact that was driven home the moment his cock head brushed against my gland and sent electric shocks through my body. "You okay?" Logan asked.

"Fuck yeah, so good. You're so damn long," I gritted out and reached for him, needing all the contact even as he pumped into me.

Logan leaned forward, bringing us chest-to-chest, never stopping the thrusting of his hips. "Never felt anything so fucking good," he panted against my lips. "So tight and hot. Wanna fill you with my cum."

His words had my balls drawing up tight. "Do it, give me everything you've got."

Logan set a steady rhythm as his hips snapped hard and fast, his dick glancing that bundle of nerves with each deep slide. "Wanna feel you come. Jack yourself," he ordered.

I gripped my already-slick cock and stroked. Picking the same rhythm of Logan's thrusts, I thumbed my slit and jerked my shaft. Logan shifted to take my mouth with his, his tongue falling into the same rhythm as my hand and his dick.

With his balls slapping against my ass, I knew I wouldn't last much longer. "Fuck, Lo, you're gonna make me blow."

"Do it, come for me," Logan murmured against my lips. "I'm so close." He shifted his rhythm, sliding even deeper with each thrust.

When he bent to bite my nipple, I was gone. My hot load shot between us, my cock throbbing in my fist as I pulsed rope after rope of my release.

"Oh, fucking shit." Logan grunted. "Oh fuck, your ass is so tight." His rhythm faltered and he gave one last thrust before throwing his head back and groaning as his cock pumped his release into the latex.

Dropping from his arms to plaster his chest against mine, Logan pressed his face against my neck as little aftershocks of orgasm rocked through both of us.

I ran my hands up and down his back, gripping his ass. "You good?"

He grunted a reply before slipping from my body and disposing of the rubber. Within seconds, he was back by my side with my damp towel.

We cleaned up and fell back into each other's arms without a single word.

As the haze of the best sex I'd ever had lifted, I couldn't help but smile. "That was fucking amazing. Thank you."

"Thank you," Logan said sleepily. "Never thought about topping when I was fantasizing, but I could definitely get used to that from time-to-time."

"I'm totally down. But maybe give me a few

days." I shifted and winced. "Jesse's gonna ask me why I'm walking all funny tomorrow."

Logan snorted. "I'm sure he'll know why." He was quiet for a while. "I want to bottom. Not tonight and not right away, but I want that with you."

"We can do whatever you want; work our way toward it."

"Thank you." Logan snuggled close to me. "Love you."

I kissed the top of his head. "Love you, too."

TEN

LOGAN

It had been a month since the night of the football game and everything that followed. I loved my jobs, loved my friends, loved my home, loved Cruz...by all rights, things were perfect and I had nothing to complain about.

And I wasn't complaining.

But something was definitely eating at me and no matter how hard I tried to ignore it, push it away, hide from it, this tiny piece of worry niggled at my head and heart.

I'd skipped two sessions with Alicia. One because I needed to work an extra shift—I felt bad that I'd had to take off for surgery, so I offered to cover for a girl whose little one had a fever.

The second session I skipped with Alicia made me feel guilty. There was no good reason for it except I wasn't ready to delve into the past and I didn't know how to voice the other bit that was bothering me.

Which was why I found myself timidly knocking at Khi's bedroom door one afternoon after I'd heard him come in and head straight to take a shower. I figured I'd given him ample time to clean up and I wanted to talk to him before Cruz got home from Jesse's.

"Come in," Khi called out.

I pushed the door open and dipped my head, suddenly even more nervous when I saw him stretched out on his bed. "Hi. Do you have a minute?"

Khi eyed me wearily but nodded and pointed toward a desk chair.

I closed the door behind me and took a seat.

"What's up?"

"Just don't lose yourself. Don't make him your life. Because when he's gone, you're the one left to pull it together and continue on your own. Don't fall so deep in with him that you have no clue who you are when you find yourself alone."

Khi's words—which had been swimming in my head day and night—came back to me. I'd tried and tried to ignore them. Tried to convince myself they didn't apply to me and Cruz. Did my best to hide from the thoughts that haunted me each time I heard those words on repeat in my head.

"What did you mean when you told me not to lose myself?" I blurted.

Khi's eyes went wide. "Hey, for real, I was exhausted and having a really down day. Don't listen to what I say. I've got so much shit going on up here," he tapped his head, "I'm the last person anyone should listen to."

"Noted. But what did you mean?" I barreled on.

He sighed. "I'm not in the mood to spill my guts, but suffice it to say that I lost myself. Fell head over heels and thought he was my forever. When he was gone, I was lost. I had no clue how to be me. Didn't know who I was anymore without him."

"Do you think that's how I am with Cruz?" I chewed on a fingernail.

Khi smiled softly. "That's not something I can answer. You two seem really happy and I can tell you both care for each other deeply." He shrugged. "Only you can answer that question. Who are you without Cruz?"

I didn't like the question and I certainly didn't like what I suspected the answer was. Pushing to my feet I quickly shoved the chair back to the desk. "Yeah, thanks. Sorry to interrupt." I yanked open the door. "I'll see you at dinner, I guess."

"Hey, Logan," Khi said softly.

Pausing at the door, I glanced back over my shoulder. "Yeah?"

"You can do both, you know? Be Logan and still have Cruz. You just have to be aware of what's happening." He shook his head and his gaze indicated he'd lost himself in a memory. "Just don't let yourself go because of him."

I gave a quick nod and closed the door, leaving Khi with his memories. I wondered if Alicia had room in her schedule for one more.

All through dinner, my shift at the Wishing Well, and cuddling in Cruz's arms later that night, Khi's words played through my head.

I needed an appointment with Alicia. Stat.

"I WAS BEGINNING to think you were ghosting me," Alicia said with a smile as she placed a mug of tea and plate of cookies in front of me. She settled in her chair with her ever-present notebook and pen. "What's up?"

She always started things so casually and I appreciated that. Hard, specific questions right up front tended to make me defensive. She knew what she was doing though, because starting our conversations with zero pressure usually led to me spilling my guts sooner rather than later.

I sipped my tea and chomped on a cookie. Sometimes I wondered if she put something in the treats that made me word-vomit all over her office. "I've got two things to discuss and both are big."

Alicia made a note and nodded. "I'm here to listen."

Taking a deep breath, I launched into my prepared argument. Even though I had a feeling Alicia would take it apart piece-by-piece, I needed to say what I was feeling. "I know you want me to talk about my past. I need to voice that I don't think it's necessary."

No shock or anger or judgement crossed Alicia's face, she simply waited.

"So, I've been thinking of it like a metaphor. Kinda. I don't know. But let's say I was stung by a bee in the past and I'm terrified of being stung again. Would you spend time and effort getting me to relive the pain of that bee sting? Or would you want to work with me so I realize not all bees are going to sting me and I don't need to be afraid?" I jutted my chin, feeling equally smug and childish for my bee sting analogy when it came to discussing my history of sexual abuse. Mainly, I wanted to convince her that opening myself to the pain of my past wasn't necessary because I was ready and willing to move on with my present and future.

Alicia scribbled something on her notebook before speaking. "I'd counter that hiding the memories of being stung would give the pain of your past more power, a power it doesn't deserve." She studied me. "I'd press that I know the pain of that bee sting is never going to truly be erased from your mind, but giving voice to the fear and pain can assist in taking away some of its power."

"But everything is good." I'd known she wouldn't go for it, but I couldn't let it go. "I'm safe, I'm working, I'm with friends, and things with Cruz are so good. Sex is amazing and has never once triggered any bad memories. I don't understand why we need to dredge up the pain of my past when it's no longer affecting me."

Alicia cocked her head. "Is it not?"

I shook my head stubbornly. "No, it's not."

"Blocking out the bad has worked well for you so far and I'm not saying it's the worst coping skill to have. But what happens when a day comes that something Cruz—or someone else—says or does brings those demons clawing to the surface and you're slapped with overwhelming pain and fear and no healthy skills to deal with it? Every step forward you've made, every sense of peace, every bit of moving on could come tumbling down around you with one triggering episode." Alicia leaned forward in her chair. "I can't and won't force this on you. But if you'll work with me, we can design a plan for if and when that happens. I want you to be prepared, equipped with ways to deal with and overcome the trigger."

I flopped back against the couch. "And what if I open up the past and experience all of that pain and then never have a triggering episode or reason to use these skills you want to teach me?"

"Honestly, I'd say that would be a win. Who's to say that working through the past and taking away its power isn't the whole reason why you won't have future triggering episodes?" Alicia tapped her pen on her notebook.

Ugh, I hated that what she said made sense.

"I'm guessing it won't be a one-and-done, talk about it and I'm all fixed type thing, right?"

Alicia smiled sadly. "You'd be correct. It will take time. I'm not going to lie and tell you it will be easy. We'll continue with the work we've been doing with reframing. I've already been introducing bits of cognitive and cognitive-behavioral therapy into our sessions, but I'd increase that with the addition of you giving a voice to the past." She leaned forward and smiled. "Revisiting the past won't be something we have to do often. I think you'll agree that once it's out, you'll be able to work through the pain, anger, and fear easier with each and every exercise." She took a sip of her own tea. "There will be stumbling points and setbacks, it's important to note that. But I wouldn't advise this if I wasn't one-hundred percent sure you're ready for it."

"I'll let you know before our next appointment, how's that?" I grumbled.

Alicia placed the pen against her lips and I got the distinct impression she was attempting to hide her smile. "I think that's a good plan and I'll be ready to support you through it."

I narrowed my eyes at her. "You're evil."

She pressed her lips together and this time I knew damn well she was fighting to hold back a smile. "You said you had two things to discuss?"

My stomach plummeted. "Yeah. The other one has to do with Cruz."

Alicia waited.

"One of my roommates has been through a really bad breakup recently and he once told me not to lose myself in Cruz. Told me to think about what would happen if I woke up and Cruz was gone, who would I be and how would I move on?" I ran my sweaty palms up and down my thighs.

"And this has been on your mind?"

"A lot. Like, constantly." I clasped my hands behind my neck.

"Why is that?"

"From the very first second Cruz came into my life, he's been my savior. I trust him with my life. But we've been inseparable from that first night. Sharing a bed, sharing a house, sharing rides to our workplace, all kinds of shit like that. He's been my constant support. Taking me to the doctor—hell, he and Bev are the only reasons I have jobs and insurance—taking me to surgery, taking me on my first date, making my first positive experiences with sex absolutely amazing." I hugged my arms around myself.

"It sounds like you have a really strong support system." Alicia studied me. "Can you voice what's bothering you?"

"If I woke up tomorrow and Cruz was gone, could I survive?"

Alicia waited.

I worried my bottom lip. "I relied on my parents and they were taken away. I relied on the foster system and it failed me. I had no choice but to rely on Lilly. She exploited me and sold me into horrors no one should have to experience." My stomach roiled. "What if," I bit my thumbnail, "what if I've moved from being trapped in one bad situation to another?"

"Do you feel trapped with Cruz? Do you feel he's using you?"

I shook my head. "Not at all and that's why these questions are driving me insane. Cruz is my savior, he's the first person I can ever remember loving and trusting a thousand percent since my parents died. He's my best friend in addition to all the rest of what he means to me."

"But?"

"But if he were to be yanked away from me, who would I be? Am I only me when I'm part of Logan and Cruz? If he was gone tomorrow, would I still have a life outside of us?" I pinched the bridge of my nose and blew out a slow breath.

"What do you feel you rely on Cruz for too much?"

"I don't know that there's specific items, but I know the thought of not having him in my life makes me feel shaky and sick, like life wouldn't be worth living." I pulled my knees to my chest.

"What are your feelings on how to proceed?" Alicia asked as she wrote something.

"I think I need some space from him. Not like a breakup," I added hastily, "just some space for me to make sure I know who Logan is without Cruz. If that makes sense?"

"And how are you predicting Cruz will react to this?"

I smiled and blinked away tears. "That's one of the reasons this is so terribly hard and why I love him so damn much. He'll support me no matter what. He'll likely be sad, but he'll work damn hard to understand and give me what I need."

"Sounds like someone worth keeping on your side," Alicia answered softly.

"Do you think I'm ridiculous for thinking I need to step back and make sure I know who Logan is?" I wanted her to tell me I was being stupid, Cruz and I were great, I had no reason to worry.

"Only you can answer that. If this is something you've been worrying about—enough to bring it up with me—it's probably worth looking into. Cruz sounds like someone who loves you, respects you, and supports you."

I ran my hands over my face and tried to push away the tears that threatened. If I was already this worried about stepping away from Cruz, what would it be like to actually do it?

"We're out of time today, but call if you need anything between now and next week. I hope your break gives you what you're looking for." Alicia clicked her pen and set aside her notebook.

I left her office knowing I was about to do

something that had the potential to backfire and break my heart. But it was also something I needed to be strong enough to do and I knew Cruz would do his best to support me. Maybe that's what love was all about. I hoped this step would end up making us stronger—I couldn't keep going on with what we had if it meant constantly wondering if I was only the man I was becoming because of Cruz. I had to prove that Logan Miles was strong, courageous, and moving on with his life with or without Cruz.

When I walked into Remington Place, Bev took one look at me and pulled me into a hug. Somehow, the woman always knew.

"You ever had to do something really hard? Something that you knew was going to hurt, but you also knew it would be worth it in the long run?" I asked.

She patted my back. "I think we've all been in that situation at least once or twice."

I took a shuddering breath. "I know it's for the best, but it's going to hurt like a bitch."

"That man loves you more than life itself and we'll all be here for you and him both. You do what Logan needs right now. The rest will work itself out." Bev patted my cheek. "But we're eating dinner first, so don't go breaking hearts until after dessert."

ELEVEN
CRUZ

"CAN WE MAYBE TAKE A WALK? Need to talk to you about something." Logan's eyes told me something was up and my nerves immediately kicked in. I had a strong feeling I wasn't going to like whatever he needed to tell me.

"Sure, grab a sweatshirt. It's chilly." I reached for my zip-up hoodie and followed Logan down the stairs.

When he went to the back door to get his sweatshirt from the hook, Bev caught my arm. "No matter what, it'll all be okay. Be there for him, he needs to know he's got your love and support even through this."

Oh, God. My stomach plummeted. Yeah, I definitely wasn't going to like this.

Logan took my hand as we descended the back

steps and headed toward the sidewalk. "I saw Alicia today."

"Yeah, how was that?"

He shrugged. "I think she's finally convinced me to go poking and prodding around in the past. I don't like it and I don't want to do it, but if it means easing the pain and fear, calming the anger—all of which I'm exhausted trying to hide and ignore—then I guess it's worth it." He squeezed my hand. "Everything I'm doing right now is to make myself healthier, better, and able to live a normal life—I know normal is relative and not the best word, but you know what I mean."

"I do." I brought his hand to my mouth and kissed his knuckles. "You know I want what's best for you, no matter what."

"I know. And that's why this is so damn fucking hard and I hate it," his voice cracked as the words spilled from him.

We'd reached the small park area at the end of Pleasure Boulevard. "I had a feeling this wasn't a recreational walk." I gestured toward the wooden bench under the big oak tree. "Let's sit and you can tell me what's going on."

Logan settled onto my lap, his legs stretched out on the bench while he cuddled into my arms. "You are so damn good to me. I'm not to a point yet where

I think I deserve your goodness, but I love you so fucking much for it."

I tipped Logan's chin and kissed him, deep and slow, our tongues entwining as I savored the taste of him. There was sadness and desperation in his kiss. Deep in my heart, I knew I needed to enjoy the contact before it was gone. Eventually, we broke for air and I pulled back. "I love you. Always. Whether we're boyfriends, friends, whatever. I'm not going anywhere."

Logan nodded and swallowed hard, tears escaping to his cheeks as he squeezed his eyes shut. "I think I need to take a break, a little space." His eyes shot open and he cupped my cheek. "Not a breakup. Unless that's what you want. I don't want to breakup." He pressed his forehead against mine. "I know it's completely unfair of me to ask for space in one breath and beg you not to break up with me in the next."

"Tell me what's going on," I whispered. "I don't want a breakup either."

"Khi said something to me the night of our first date and I've not been able to get it out of my head."

I cocked a brow. "Khi?" Gee, thanks man.

"I spoke to him about it again—when I couldn't make the thoughts go away—and he explained a bit more." Logan shifted and leaned his head against my shoulder. "He didn't give a lot of details, but he went through a really bad breakup. I guess he'd basically devoted his entire being to this guy and when it ended, Khi was lost. Had no clue who he was outside of the relationship, no idea how to pick up and move on. He advised me to not lose myself and to never forget who I am outside of Logan and Cruz."

"And you think you're lost in us?" My heart hurt saying the words, but I also understood where he was coming from. Hell, sometimes I felt lost in us and I had several years of experience on him. I'd had time to move on from my shitty past, find a place to settle, learn a bit about who I was before Logan came into my life.

Logan? He'd looked up from a beating on the dirty ground of an alley to see me and we'd been attached at the hip ever since. I'd had concerns that what we fell into wasn't the healthiest relationship—I'd just been too chicken shit to bring it up. Didn't want to upset him, didn't want to lose him, didn't want to admit that maybe I needed to step back from being everything to him.

And here he was, my strong, courageous Logan, recognizing our missteps and taking action to make them right. God, I loved him so damn much.

Logan nodded. "Sometimes? I don't know. I don't know what to think. I think I love you more than life itself. I trust you with my whole being; you're my savior, my safe space, my person."

"But?"

"But if you walked away tomorrow, who would I be?"

I hugged him close. "I get what you're saying. I really do. No matter what, I want you to know that I'm not walking away unless you tell me that's what you need."

Logan shook his head vigorously. "No. Not even close to what I need. Honestly, the only reason I'm confident in taking this step back and giving myself a little space is because I know you love me and you'll support me." A frown creased his brow. "Which is so damn selfish of me..."

"Hey, no. Don't do that. It's not selfish. I've told you from the very beginning, even before I was in love with you, that I'd be here. I've never really understood the instant, strong connection between us, but I'm not giving up on it." I kissed the top of his head.

"You're taking all of this very well," Logan hedged.

"I don't like it and it hurts to think of not being around you as much—or whatever it is you think needs to happen—but I can't lie and say I don't think it's a fairly solid idea."

"You think we're lost in each other?" Logan scowled. "I get that it's immature of me to be the one to bring up this idea and then pout when you agree with it, but I don't like that you also think we need time apart. If we both think we need a break, what's to say we'll ever find our way back to each other?"

"I don't think we're both lost. I don't even think you're lost." I tipped his chin and brushed a kiss over his lips, trying to gather as many as possible before the inevitable. "I think that maybe I stepped in and took over too much. Maybe I've become some sort of knight in shining armor for you." I kissed his temple and breathed in deeply. "While I love being there for you, I think you might be right that you need to find Logan outside of Logan and Cruz." I ran a hand up and down his arm. "We'll find our way back to each other for a couple reasons."

Logan glanced up, waiting.

"One, are you moving away from Remington?"

He shook his head.

"Right. Neither am I. We'll figure out how to work the sleeping arrangements." I held up two fingers. "Two, are you going to distance yourself from our friends? Stop eating Bev's dinners?"

He smiled softly, love shining from his eyes. "No."

"Same." I added a third finger. "Third, I love you to the moon and back and I think you feel the same. We'll find our way back to each other because we're not going anywhere and what we have is too special to let it get away."

Logan took a deep shuddery breath as tears streamed down his cheeks. "Thank you. Thank you for being you, for understanding me, for your unwavering love and support."

My heart broke to pieces as I held him and let him cry.

"So, how are we going to do this? Set a time limit? Rules?" I didn't want to set the plan in motion, but it seemed as if the sooner we took the step, the sooner we could get back to Logan and Cruz. I wasn't sure I needed the space as badly as Logan, but I had a feeling that the break—while painful—wouldn't be a bad thing for me.

"I can find a place to stay…"

I interrupted him. "No. I'll stay with Jesse and Cooper. They have a basement. You can have our room and stay with Bev and the crew."

"It was your room first," Logan argued.

"I'm not budging on this one."

He sighed. "Okay. Thank you. I don't think a set time limit is needed. I think I'll know when I'm supposed to know."

"Okay." I pressed my lips against his temple. "Wish we knew how long that would be because I'm kinda gonna hate sleeping without you."

"I know," he whispered. "I have some thoughts on things I need to do while we're giving each other space. The main thing I have to know is that I can survive and thrive without you if needed." Logan cupped my face and kissed me, long and slow. When we broke apart, his words were heavy with emotion. "Please know that I never want to have to live without you, I just need to know that I could. Based on how this relationship came together, I never really got the chance to know me without you." He huffed. "I don't know if that even makes sense."

I nodded. "It does." A thought struck me and I immediately hated it.

Logan must have noticed the way I tensed. "What's wrong?"

"I think one of the things you need to do is go out without me."

He cocked his head. "Like with our friends? Yeah, I figured Cooper and Rai and I could hang out a bit more if they have time. We're close in age and I get along with them really well."

I swallowed thickly. "Yeah, that's a good idea. But not what I meant."

Logan wrinkled his nose. "I don't get it, go out

without…" Dawning lit his face. "Oh my God, you mean like date?"

I closed my eyes and gritted my teeth. "At least one date."

"But…why? Do you want me to find someone else?" Logan's words belied his emotions.

"No. Never. But you've never dated before me. We've agreed that maybe our relationship borders a bit on codependency."

Logan pulled back as if he'd been slapped and I held up a hand.

"I'm not saying we're codependent in the actual definition of the word, but I think we both can admit that taking this break could lead to a healthier relationship. Right?"

Logan's shoulders drooped. "Yeah, you're right." He gave me a pouty look. "It really sucks that you're so on board with this. Makes me think you want out."

"Do you want out?" I countered.

"Of course not."

"I don't either. But you came to me with a concern and I won't lie and say it's not something I've had my own concerns about. If we're going to do this, I think it's best if we're on the same page and approaching it as a strategy to strengthen what we have."

Logan nodded. "I don't understand why you want me to date someone else."

"I don't want you to date someone else." The words were like gravel in my throat. "But I think it's a good idea. Logan outside of Logan and Cruz needs to have experiences that don't include me."

His eyes went wide and I recognized panic. "I will not have sex with anyone else, Cruz, I can't. I don't know why it works so well with you and sends me into a tailspin to even think about it with others outside of my fantasies, but I just can't."

I held him tighter. "I wouldn't expect you to or want you to, unless it was something you needed. I'm just saying, have at least one date so I'm not the only person you've gone out with." I tipped his chin. "Because—and I need you to hear this loud and clear—when this break is over, you're coming back to me for good. So, you better plan on finding yourself and figuring out what you need to figure out. I will never let you go again."

Logan chuckled through tears and kissed me soundly. "I'm going to take that in the loving promise way rather than the creepy way."

I smiled against his lips. "Yeah, it was meant as a loving promise, not creepy. Sorry."

"So, being on a break...means? We don't sleep in the same bed or share a room for the time being.

Maybe I go on a date. I don't want to force it. What else?" Logan cuddled back into my arms.

"What do you need from this time?" I still hated the thought of it and knew I'd hate every moment of it, but I knew Logan needed it.

"I'm going to spend a lot of time journaling and thinking about what I need and want from life. I want to look into helping at the homeless shelter. I want to cook with Bev, help with Hadley, and discover my new town—like taking walks and coming across hidden treasures I didn't know existed. I want to go to lunch and a movie by myself —okay, if I'm being honest, the thought of that is terrifying and I don't want to, but I'm going to. I'm going to go shopping with Cooper and buy clothes just because I like them. I'm going to let Dre design something for me." The words rushed from Logan in a jumble and when he paused with a smile, I knew this step was exactly what he needed even though I hated it. His eyes went wide. "I want to learn to drive."

My stomach clenched because I knew he'd always been afraid of driving. "I can help."

He cocked his head and pressed a kiss to my cheek. "I know you can and you would in a heartbeat. But I need to do this on my own."

"Right." I sighed. "I think stepping back and not helping is going to be hard for me."

He smiled. "I know it will be. That's just who you are and I love you for it. Give me a bit of time, we'll be back in our own bed and I'll be letting you help me all you want."

"So, I'm thinking this break should probably mean no sex, yeah?" I linked our fingers together.

Logan sighed. "Yeah, probably for the best. Is it strange that I'll miss the sex like crazy, but I'll miss just being with you and in your arms even more?"

My chest constricted. "Not strange because I feel exactly the same way. Honestly, no idea how I'm going to let you go." I wrapped him in a tighter embrace.

"Is it any easier knowing it's temporary and to make us better?"

"If it wasn't, I don't think I'd survive it." I shifted him in my arms. "We should head back. I need to pack and ask Jesse if I can stay in his basement before it gets too late."

Logan stayed cuddled under my arm the whole way back to Remington Place.

"I'll meet you upstairs. Gonna ask Jesse first." I let him go at the gate and watched him walk up the back steps before going to Jesse's side door. I knocked and waited.

When Jesse swung the door open, the night must have shown on my face because he immediately stepped back to let me in. "What happened?"

I broke and found myself gathered up in Jesse's arms. "Logan needs a break," I choked out.

Cooper appeared at our side and rubbed a hand up and down my back as I gave a brief Cliff Notes version of what was going on.

"The worst part is I know it's for the best, but damn, I'm going to miss him." I sniffed and wiped my eyes as I stepped away from Jesse's hug. "Um, any chance I could stay in the basement while Logan sorts himself out?"

"Of course, that's not a problem at all. Glad to help." Jesse reached for a row of keys hanging by the door. "Here's a copy of the house key so you can come and go as you please. Anything you need, just ask." He put an arm around Cooper. "For what it's worth, I think it's probably the best thing for you guys right now. He loves you very much and I think your relationship will be stronger and better after this."

I sighed. "I know and I agree. That's what sucks so much. I know it needs to be done, I just hate the path to get there."

"We'll be here for both of you, promise. I'll be sure to be around for bro time as much as possible—

Logan always seemed to be missing out on that experience. Maybe Rai and I can take him shopping and have a few days together doing whatever." Cooper snuggled into Jesse's side.

When I noticed they were both shirtless and in their pajama bottoms, I winced. "Sorry for showing up late. I know you guys don't get a lot of private time and I interrupted."

"Nah, we were just watching TV. We'll do that a little later." Cooper winked. "No worries, the basement is very soundproof."

I laughed. "I'm going to run over and pack. Thank you for letting me stay. Wasn't sure where I'd go if you said no."

"Never. We're family." Jesse gestured toward the basement door. "Light switch at the top of the stairs turns it on, you can flip it off at the bottom. Bathroom is stocked. There are sheets and pillows and blankets in the closet. The whole place is yours for as long as you need it."

I told the guys goodnight and promised to lock the door behind me when I returned before heading to Remington Place.

Bev met me in the kitchen and wrapped me in a hug. "It's going to work out, I just know it. Don't you be a stranger during this time or I'll come drag you by your ear back here."

I chuckled. "Yes, ma'am." I kissed her cheek. "I'm gonna pack. Jesse and Cooper said I could stay with them for a while."

"I expect you here for dinner and breakfast as usual. Lunch if you need it." Bev patted my arm. "It's hard, but it's a good move on his part. Wasn't sure he had it in him, but he proved me wrong."

Taking a deep shuddering breath, I smiled. "He's the strongest person I know. I'm blessed to know him."

"Pretty sure he feels the same about you. You two are a match I didn't see coming, but it's a good one and I'll be on the sidelines cheering you on. A relationship is best when both people know and love themselves in addition to knowing and loving their partner." Bev said goodnight before making her way to her bedroom.

When I reached our room, I found Logan crying. "Hey, we're good." I tipped his chin and met his eyes. "This is good. It hurts, but it's for the best."

"I love you, please don't ever think I don't," Logan whispered as he wrapped arms around my neck.

"The only way I can face this is knowing you love me." I ran a thumb over his lip before I devoured his mouth in the sweetest, most promising kiss in the history of kisses.

Logan sat somberly on the bed as I threw clothes in a bag. "Can we still text?"

"I'd be disappointed if we didn't."

When I stood near the door, ready to head to Jesse's, Logan popped up and rummaged through his old backpack. He kissed the top of Bunny's head and thrust the old stuffed animal at me. "Bunny will keep you company and make sure you don't forget me."

I laughed through the tightness in my throat. "As if that could ever happen. But I'll be glad to have Bunny by my side." I tucked the rabbit under my arm and pulled Logan close. "Never forget how much I love you. This is a good move and we'll be stronger because of it. When you come back to me, there's no looking back." I pressed a hard kiss against his mouth. When we broke apart, both teary, we pressed our foreheads together and just savored the moment. "You're my world, Logan. I want to give you everything you need, but I need you back in my arms. As soon as possible."

"I love you so much," Logan choked out on a sob. "I'll be back, no way you're getting rid of me. Thank you for understanding and giving me this."

I left Logan and made my way down the stairs and to Jesse's basement in a fog of sadness. Tossing my bag to the ground, I collapsed on the couch and finally let loose the sobs that had threatened for the past hour.

THE NEXT MONTH was excruciating and I hated every single moment of it.

Except when I saw Logan smiling, growing, making huge strides, and becoming the man he wanted to be. I didn't hate those moments.

And luckily, they happened often.

Logan and I were blessed with amazing friends—found family was the word I'd use for them—and they stood by our sides through the entire break.

While Rai was introducing Logan to the game shop and inviting him to gaming nights, he was also filling me in on how much fun Logan was having with new friends.

While Dalton and Gabby were talking financial shit with Logan, helping him set up a savings account and pick the best credit card for him, they were also reporting to me that he was determined to set himself up for a successful future.

When Cooper took Logan shopping and out to lunch, he also made sure to let me know that Logan mentioned certain outfits he wanted to wear on dates with me.

After Jesse spent an entire day teaching Logan how to check his oil and fluids, change a flat, jump a dead battery, and change his filters and oil, he sat with me in the basement and made sure I knew exactly how unfaltering Logan was about getting himself on track and back to me.

When Dre excitedly designed an entire outfit for Logan to wear on his birthday, he made it a point to let me know Logan talked incessantly about the strides he was making with Alicia and how much he loved me.

Every time Spencer came back from teaching Logan how to drive, he made sure to stop by the shop to fill me in on Logan's progress and how proud he was of himself.

Every single one of our friends spent time with Logan, letting him know he was valued and loved, yet they never once stopped making sure I knew that the break was just a stepping stone and eventually we'd be back together.

Even Khi, after apologizing if his words had played a part in the separation, took to texting me and letting me know how Logan was doing.

I worked hard at savoring both the little updates and the chances to see Logan spread his wings and step out on his own, but I had a harder time staying busy than he appeared to. I worked overtime at the shop, took extra shifts at the Wishing Well, and started playing games and watching videos with Hadley.

Logan and I were still in contact and friendly. We texted daily, saw each other at Thursday dinners and most days at breakfast, and I usually caught a glimpse or two of him at the Wishing Well.

He always had that special smile just for me.

His eyes always caught mine and reminded me of why we were paused for a moment.

And he kept me updated on his progress with Alicia.

"I'm really glad we took a moment," he told me one night after dinner as we sat on the back steps. "The shit Alicia has me working through is rough and I definitely think it would have been a step backwards in our sex life."

I took his hand—I'd never been able to stop holding his hand and he didn't seem to mind—and gave it a squeeze. "Even if there are obstacles when we're back on track, that's okay. I'm not in this just for the sex."

Logan leaned his head against my shoulder. "I know and I love you for it."

"Love you, too. And I'm so damn proud of you."

He looked up and smiled. "I'm proud of me, too. And that's something I don't ever remember. I've

never felt proud of myself—at least not since before
the wreck. But I am. I'm proud as fuck of all the shit
I'm working through, all the shit I'm learning, and
the person I've become."

I pulled him close and kissed the top of his head.
"You don't need me—never did and never will—to
be an amazing man. You're one of the strongest,
most courageous, persistent people I've ever met.
With or without me, you're going to be so damn
good."

Logan smiled and hooked his arm through mine.
"That night in the alley? If you'd said those words to
me, I would have laughed in your face and spent the
night curled in a ball believing nothing but the worst
was what I deserved." He laced our fingers. "But
now? I'm this close to believing every word you just
said."

I cleared my throat. "So, I hear you've got a date
tomorrow night?" I wanted to punch a wall. Wanted
to scream. Wanted to destroy something. But this
was an important step and Logan needed to know.

He wrinkled his nose. "Yeah. I'm kinda worried
because the guy is super nice and Cooper really likes
him—says he's an amazing teacher and all-around
great guy."

I needed to puke. "Sounds great."

"It would be easier to let him down easy if he was

a jerk. I don't want to make him feel bad when I tell him I can't go on a second date with him because the man I'm madly in love with is the only person I want to date and spend the rest of my life with." Logan propped his chin on his hand and studied me. "I'm mostly doing this date thing for you, you know?"

"And I'm kicking myself for even suggesting it," I grumbled.

"I can cancel. I don't need a date with Scott to know that I love you."

I shook my head. "No, I think it's important in the long run. Even if it's just one date, I think you need to be able to look back and say you tried things, gave it your best effort, that kind of thing."

Logan sighed. "It's kinda shitty to let Scott take me on a date when I have no intention of continuing the relationship beyond one friendly date."

"Does he know about me?"

He nodded. "I've let him know what's going on. He's not looking to settle down and he's fairly new in town, so he was game to just go out as friends basically." Logan bumped my shoulder. "And don't even mention sex or anything. I'm not at that point with anyone but you." He put a hand up when I started to protest. "And before you say that maybe someday I will be, just stop. Alicia agrees that it's very likely you're the only person I'll ever feel comfortable developing sexual feelings toward. And it's okay. You've been my safe space since day one. Whether I'm learning to be me outside of us or not, you've continued to be my safe space and the only person I can imagine being intimate with."

I gave a nod and ignored the fire in my chest. "It's a damn privilege to be that for you and I never want to screw it up."

I gave Logan a quick hug and a kiss on the forehead and said goodnight before beelining it to Jesse's basement and spending the night tossing and turning thinking about how much I loved Logan and the fact that he was going out with another man the next night.

By the time I finished at the shop on Friday evening, I'd nearly given myself an ulcer and wished like hell someone, anyone would have needed me to cover their shift at the bar. But I was free for the entire night with nothing to do except think about Logan on a date with Scott.

"Carry-out and beer?" Jesse asked as we cleaned up.

"Fuck, yes. Please. Many, many beers."

He laughed. "Figured as much. Hadley's with Bev tonight so we have all night to drink and shoot the shit. I'll build a fire out back."

"Sounds perfect. Thanks, man."

"No worries. Get cleaned up. I'll call in an order."

Thirty minutes later, as I walked out the side door of Jesse's house, I caught a glimpse of a silver car pulling up in front of Remington Place. My gut clenched and I knew I should look away, but I found myself frozen in place as I watched an extremely attractive man, probably about twenty-six-ish, climb from the car and head up the front steps.

Damn right he better go to the front door to pick him up. Didn't bring flowers, though. Logan deserves flowers.

A few moments later, Logan's laugh carried through the air as he followed Scott to the car.

Look away, stupid.

But I couldn't.

Logan looked absolutely delectable in a pair of stylishly ripped jeans, a tight red t-shirt, a black sweater, and a scarf.

Damn, your boy cleans up nice.

Fuck yeah, he did.

"If it helps," Cooper stage-whispered from my side, nearly causing me a heart attack, "those clothes are borrowed from me. He refused to wear any of his new stuff until he can go on a date with you."

I turned toward Cooper just as Logan glanced our way. "Really?"

Cooper nodded.

"Well, it doesn't help at all to see him climbing in a car with some other guy, but that tidbit does offer a little reassurance," I grumbled. By the time I tossed a quick look over my shoulder, the silver car was gone, but Jesse's truck was rumbling up.

"Come on, let's eat a ton of greasy food, drink until we're nearly sick, and forget about heartache for the night." Cooper hooked his arm in mine and led me toward the firepit.

Three hours later, I was stuffed on burgers, fries, and amazing donut balls Jesse had bought. Oh, and lots of beer. Lots and lots of beer.

We'd done absolutely nothing but eat, drink, and laugh our asses off all night and it was the most perfect way to spend the evening trying to forget the man I loved was out on a date with another guy.

"Would it help if I told you that Scott is really nice and good? He knows the score, he's not looking for anything more than friendship right now, and he'd never try to take advantage of Logan." Cooper placed a hand on my arm as firelight cast orange shadows and I stared toward the street as if I could will Logan to get home.

"Not really. That just makes me realize that Scott is likely ten times better for Logan than I could ever be," I groused, the beer buzz making me grumpy and melancholy at the same time. I wanted Logan in my arms, wanted the damn break to be over and done with. Instead, I was stuck sleeping with a damn stuffed bunny every night and jacking off by myself every morning.

"Don't say that. I've spent a lot of time with Logan—before and during this break—and I can assure you that no one makes his eyes light up the way you do. You and he have clicked from that very first night." Cooper handed me another beer and I swore it needed to be my last. "It's been a month of Logan spreading his wings, but there's not been a single moment when it's not been perfectly clear that, while he's doing this for himself, he's also doing it for your relationship. That man loves you with every fiber of his being. No one is better for him than you."

I glanced at Jesse to see if he agreed with what Cooper was saying. He shrugged. "Sometimes, I think Cooper gets a little too dramatic and romanticizes things a bit much…"

Cooper gasped and feigned offense.

Jesse just laughed. "But, in this case, I can't help but agree with him. You and Logan may not understand the why around it, but you just click. You complement each other and fit together like no two people I've ever seen."

"Except for us, of course," Cooper added.

Jesse snorted. "Yes, of course."

We finished our beers and I finally breathed a sigh of relief when Scott's silver car pulled up in front of Remington Place.

Will he kiss him?

"Oh God, do you think he'll kiss him? I'm gonna be sick." I held my spinning head in my hands.

Cooper stood and peeked over the fence. "They're standing at the curb. Logan is showing no signs of affection or wanting a kiss. Ahh, that's sweet…"

"What? What are they doing?" I lifted my head, but didn't want to watch.

"Scott offered a handshake but Logan gave him a very friend-like hug. This is good for them, they both need friends." Cooper watched a bit longer. "Okay, they've said goodnight and Logan went inside. Case closed."

I let out a breath I didn't realize I'd been holding and stood, swaying marvelously and hiccupping. "Fuck, this is going to hurt like a bitch tomorrow."

Jesse and Cooper, somehow both a lot more sober than me, helped me to the basement where I promptly crashed into a beer-enhanced sleep until I woke feeling like death the next morning.

TWELVE

LOGAN

A COUPLE WEEKS after my date with Scott, I was about ready to jump out of my skin with impatience and longing.

The date had proved a couple things.

One, despite how much I tried to picture myself with someone like Scott, I just couldn't do it. Cruz was the only man I wanted to spend time with outside of my friends.

Two, I was absolutely miserable.

Okay, that wasn't completely true. On one hand, I was elated with all I was learning and the growth I was experiencing—I was really proud of myself and felt stronger every single day.

But on the other hand, I missed Cruz like crazy.

When we started our break, I'd told him I didn't

think we needed a specific timeline because I'd know when I was ready.

And I was ready.

Or at least I thought I was ready.

But I kept questioning everything.

Was I giving in too quickly? Would going back to what we had—was that even possible now?—going to override all of the hard work I'd been doing? Would Cruz even like the man I was becoming?

Alicia and I had made huge strides in recent sessions and, while I'd never be rid of my past and the pain it held, I was equipped with coping strategies for the day-to-day and if something were to trigger my past trauma.

I felt strong and Alicia assured me that she'd made note of several positive changes in me.

What if those changes made me into someone Cruz no longer loved?

When I'd voiced that concern to Alicia she'd cocked her head and studied me. "You're still Logan. You've gotten stronger, more independent, and better able to handle what life throws your way, but you're still the man he fell in love with."

"What if he only liked me when I needed him?" I'd asked.

Alicia waited patiently until I answered myself.

"If he only liked me when I needed him then it's

good that I've learned to live without him. I love him, but I can be strong whether in a relationship or on my own." I hated the words, but I knew they were true.

Alicia had just smiled and told me she'd see me at my next session.

I took a deep breath as I put Bev's car in reverse and backed out of the parking spot at the animal shelter. I'd just given my two-week notice—I'd no longer be on their payroll, but I'd still be coming to volunteer as much as possible.

It wasn't an easy decision, but I was in the process of reorganizing my employment because I'd just the day before learned I'd landed a part-time spot at the homeless shelter where I really wanted to be focusing a lot of my efforts. With hard work and luck, I'd get the next full-time position available. I wanted to be part of helping people find a safe spot to stay and setting them up with needed resources for their future potential success.

For the time being, I could stay on at the library and continue helping Cooper at the preschool, but those positions would have to go if I got the job I wanted at the shelter.

I wasn't quitting the Wishing Well, but I'd talked to the manager about trying to get me on shifts that weren't with Cruz. She'd looked at me kinda funny, but I didn't elaborate because it wasn't really her business. I figured part of making sure I had time outside of our relationship should probably include not spending every waking moment around each other. So separate shifts seemed like a good plan.

Honestly, I hated it because I wanted to spend as much time with Cruz as possible. However, I knew that it was too easy to fall back into being lost and not knowing who I was outside of us, so I was taking Khi's advice and just being aware. If that meant not working alongside Cruz, I could deal.

I pulled into one of the few spots at Alicia's little house-turned-office and breathed a sigh of relief before turning off the car. Spencer had been wonderful in helping me learn to drive, but it still made me slightly nervous. Between him helping with the physical driving test preparation and Rai helping me study for the written test, I'd passed with flying colors and was now the proud owner of a driver's license.

Thanks to Bev, I had a vehicle to borrow as needed—although, I often opted to walk if possible —but I had plans for purchasing my own car very soon.

Alicia smiled and waved me in when I entered the little cottage-style home she'd turned into her practice. "Your tea and cookies await." She gestured toward the room we met in most often. "And I have something to tell you."

"I'm cured? You're kicking me out? There's nothing more you can do for me and you need my spot for someone else?" I teased and we both laughed.

"No, nothing like that." Alicia sat down in her chair and grabbed her notebook.

"Thank God." I reached for a cookie. "Where else would I get my cookie and tea fix?"

We chatted a bit over our hot drinks and treats. Alicia had become a trusted confidant through all of our difficult sessions. She was still a therapist, not a friend, but we enjoyed each other's company and had plenty to talk about even when we weren't discussing my life.

"So, what's this thing you need to tell me?" I crossed a leg over my knee and tried to look professional as if I were the therapist.

Alicia smirked. "Nice try." She opened her notebook and turned to the page she was looking for. "I've gathered information about Lilly."

My stomach dropped and I feared my cookies and tea were coming back up. "Oh God, I had no clue what you were going to say, but that wasn't what I was expecting."

Alicia smiled patiently. "Would you like the details?"

"Yes? No. No, but yes. Are they bad? Like bad for me?" I leaned forward and held my head in my hands. Muttering to myself, I ran a hand through my hair. "Okay, this information is something I can't change. Whether it's good or bad isn't the point. I will deal with whatever I learn. But knowing can help relieve some of the anxiety of always wondering. Not everything is bad news. Listen to what she has to say."

Alicia waited through my little self-talk. When I took a deep breath and sat up straight, giving her a nod, she smiled. "That was good. You ready?"

I swallowed thickly, worried that what she had to tell me was going to set me back a million years, but choked out, "Yes."

"It took a bit of digging—and calling in a few favors from some friends I can't mention—but I found some details. Lilly Gregory didn't die the day you pushed her. From the 911 call that was made, it appears as if she eventually dragged herself to the door and got outside. A neighbor found her and called for help."

She didn't die.

I wasn't a murderer.

But she didn't die.

Lilly was still preying on kids.

Talk about a good news, bad news situation.

"There's more," Alicia continued. "The information is murky as to how and why the authorities got involved, but they did. Lilly was—unbeknownst to her and maybe not for the first time—put on a watchlist. Eventually, about a year and a half after you and Rusty got out, she was arrested and one of the largest trafficking rings in the country was busted."

My eyes grew wide. "For real? She was caught? Punished?"

Alicia nodded. "I don't know about all of the pieces who had a part in the ring, but Lilly was charged with several counts of trafficking and sexual abuse. From what I'm told, even if only half of the charges ended in prison time, she'll spend the rest of her life locked up." A frown marred Alicia's forehead. "If she survives prison. I'm under the impression that she's in an area not known for leniency from other inmates when word gets out about crimes against children."

"So, she's alive and in prison now and likely will die there?"

Alicia nodded. "It's been about a year and a half since her arrest and many of the court proceedings are still taking place, but she's serving time during all of that. My understanding is that she's been assaulted more than once by her fellow inmates."

I winced. "Wow, what a brain fuck. I wanted her dead, but I didn't want to be the one who killed her. She's not dead, but getting assaulted behind bars. Damn, I feel guilty for being a bit disappointed she's not dead and even guiltier for being glad she's being taken care of in prison." I clasped my hands behind my neck. "Am I a bad person for taking satisfaction in knowing she's being hurt maybe a fraction of the ways she made me hurt?"

Alicia shook her head. "Not at all. It's a natural reaction."

"Wow." I took a deep breath. "I don't think I'd realized how much not knowing was eating at me. You think the dreams about that day will stop now?"

"Maybe. You never know. Dreams are hard to pin down."

We spent the next half-hour working through some exercises before calling it quits and making my next appointment. I was on an every two-week schedule now and we were slowly working toward monthly. Alicia assured me I'd eventually be able to check-in every three to six months, but she wasn't pushing for it just yet.

"So, I'm thinking of ending the break with Cruz,"

I said nonchalantly as I put the next appointment in my phone.

"Yeah?"

"Any suggestions for how to make myself believe I'm ready?"

"Do you feel ready? Does it feel right?" Alicia cocked her head.

"Yes. But my head keeps telling me that maybe I'm still too reliant on him."

"So, make a list. You know how writing things down and making lists has helped you in previous sessions. Do that now. What can you do without Cruz? What can you not do without Cruz? If the list shows you need Cruz—meaning you're truly unable to do those things on your own—then maybe you need more time apart." She glanced at her phone. "I've got a lunch date with my husband. Go make your list and I'll see you in two weeks."

As I turned toward the door, Alicia stopped me.

"Logan?"

I glanced back at her.

"Remember, it's not a bad thing to rely on someone from time-to-time. I know your reasons for wanting to be independent and not lose yourself in the relationship and they're solid reasons, especially based on your past experiences. Just don't lose out on something good because of a false belief that you're weak if you need support."

"That's good advice, thanks. You should be like a therapist or something," I teased.

Alicia laughed as she waved me out the door.

I walked to Bev's car feeling light as air. I didn't kill Lilly. She was locked away and getting exactly what she deserved. And I had a plan for making my way back to Cruz.

Would he be willing to take me back?

A WEEK LATER, after spending days upon days fretting over my list and arguing with my head and heart, I paced outside of Jesse's house staring at the rumpled piece of paper in my hands.

It was the final list I'd made and there wasn't a single thing in the Need Cruz column. I mean, admittedly, having sex with Cruz was something I needed Cruz for, but it seemed redundant to put that in the column.

Every other thing I'd come up with—some that I'd previously thought I needed help with and some that I'd just never thought about—were in the Don't Need Cruz column.

The list was long and it blurred before my eyes.

Learning to drive.

Getting a job.

Changing a tire.

Making friends.

Going to lunch on my own.

Going to a movie on my own.

Getting my license.

Going on a date.

Facing my past.

Buying clothes.

Going to the doctor by myself.

Cooking a meal.

Sleeping alone.

The list went on and on. Some of the points were more serious than others, but the fact was, there wasn't a single thing—yeah, yeah, aside from sex with Cruz—that I needed him for. Did I want to have him there? Hell, yes.

I'd lucked out with great friends to support me through this time.

But even without the crew to help me, I could do everything on my own if needed. It was as if a weight was lifted off my shoulders and I could take a real breath for the first time in nearly two months.

I was me. I was Logan. Did I want more than anything to be part of Logan and Cruz? Fuck, yeah.

But if Cruz was out of the picture, could I rely on myself? Yes.

It was no longer a hesitant yes, I knew I could survive without Cruz—I could survive without needing anyone. And that confidence was the piece I'd been waiting on.

I knocked on the door and grinned as a very excited Cooper swung it open. "Oh my God, bitch, I've been waiting forever for you to knock. I thought you were going to pace out there all night." He leaned close. "Is this a reunion visit or just a booty call?"

I laughed. "Reunion. If he'll have me."

"Oh, he'll have you. I'm thinking you two should stay in the basement tonight. I know how thin the walls are at Bev's. The basement is fairly soundproof so you two can go at it all you want and no one will be the wiser." Cooper bounced on the balls of his feet. "I mean, Jesse and I will know, but not because we can hear you. No worries though, just the thought of you two fucking each other's brains out is enough to have me climbing my man like a tree so it's all good. Go at it all night long. We won't care because we'll be busy."

Jesse came around the corner. "She needed three stories and two drinks tonight. What's got you all worked up?"

Cooper wrapped his arms around Jesse's middle. "Logan is here to reunite with his one true love and they're going to bang all night which has me all kinds of horny and thinking of all the ways I want to reunite your cock with my ass…"

Jesse clamped a hand over Cooper's mouth. "Oh my God, that mouth. Sorry, Logan, don't mind him. Please, feel free to head to the basement. Feel free to stay as long as you'd like and make yourself comfortable. I'll be taking Cooper to bed."

Cooper must have licked Jesse's hand because the older man jerked his arm away and glared at Cooper before wiping his hand down his shirt.

Cooper leaned in close and pretended to whisper. "By make yourself comfortable he's politely telling you that it's okay to fuck each other until the sun comes up. When he says he's taking me to bed that's old man speak meaning he's going to bone me so hard I won't be able to walk tomorrow. Maybe not even the next day."

"Say goodnight, Cooper," Jesse ordered.

"Goodnight, Cooper," my blond friend mimicked before cackling and giving me a wave. "Love you. You've got this. He's all yours."

I made my way to the basement stairs as Jesse herded Cooper up the stairs.

Locking the door behind me, I crept down the carpeted steps.

Cruz was stretched out on the couch watching something on the TV and didn't seem to notice my approach. When I got closer, my movements caught his eye and he jumped with a yelp. "Holy shit, Lo! You scared me to death."

"Sorry," I said with a chuckle.

"Everything okay?" he asked as he shifted on the couch and made room for me.

"Yeah, things are good. Really good. Can we talk?" I sat next to him, loving that his hand immediately reached for mine.

"Always."

Cruz and I had kept in contact throughout the whole break and he probably knew about as much going on in my life as Alicia, but we'd kept things platonic throughout everything. Neither of us had felt like we could keep our level of intimacy and still call it a break.

"I made a list. The point was to see what I can do by myself and what I need you for."

"And what do you need me for?" Cruz brushed a kiss against my temple.

"Absolutely nothing," I told him with a huge smile.

He winced. "Gee, that's great, Lo." He pretended

to be hurt, but I knew he was joking. "For real, though. That's so good and I'm so proud of you. I knew you'd finally realize how strong you are. I want to be by your side, supporting you and helping you, but you don't need me. There's not a single thing you could ever want to do that you'd need me for."

"Agreed." I slid the folded paper into my jeans pocket.

"So, what does this mean?" Cruz asked, his voice gruff and filled with hope.

"It means I'm ready to call it quits." I realized how that sounded and yelped. "Call it quits on the break!" I amended. "I want you to come home."

Cruz grinned, ear-to-ear, as he wrapped me in a hug. Reaching behind me, he grabbed something and brushed it against my ear. "Can Bunny come home, too?"

I nuzzled my nose against Bunny's soft fur. "Awww, Bunny. Yes, he can come home. I've missed him most of all," I teased.

"You're still a mouthy brat, I see."

"And you're almost two months closer to your AARP card."

"God, I've missed you so damn much," Cruz whispered before cupping my face and devouring my mouth.

Several moments later, when we finally broke apart,

I bit my lip and laced our fingers together. "You know, there is one thing on the list of things I need you for."

Cruz cocked a brow. "Yeah?"

I nodded. "Mmhm, it's really hard to have sex with my boyfriend when you're not around."

"So, that's it, huh? I've been reduced to one column on a list and it's only for sexual favors?" Cruz fell back on the couch and pulled me with him.

"I'm an independent man now, babe. Take it or leave it." I pressed my hands against his chest and rocked my hips against his.

"Mmmm, take it. I want you any way I can get you," Cruz murmured before clasping my neck and yanking me close for a soul-searing, hot, and full-of-promise kiss.

"Cooper suggested we stay here tonight," I said.

"It's almost sound proof, I like that idea."

"I didn't bring clothes, I'll have to do the walk of shame back home tomorrow."

"But I'll be walking by your side." Cruz pressed a kiss to the corner of my mouth. "Not because you need me there, but because I want to be there."

I took a deep breath. "One of the things I'd been fretting over was my sexual health. It wasn't something I brought up a lot, but I ended up talking to Alicia about it"

Cruz's eyes never left mine and he held both of my hands. "I want you healthy for your sake, but no matter your status, nothing changes how I feel about you."

I smiled and pressed my forehead against his. "I know and that's why I love you so damn much. One of the things I did while we were apart was get a full physical—all the bloodwork and tests and everything. Results came back all negative. I'll see the doctor at least once a year for checkups."

Cruz brushed a kiss over my mouth. "Great minds and all that. I also took our little break to get a physical—I mean, my sexy, mouthy boyfriend was off spreading his wings and finding himself, what else was I to do with my time than get bloodwork?" He nuzzled my nose when I laughed. "My results came back negative."

"Did you get a colonoscopy? Isn't that something guys your age are supposed to get?" I bit my lip and tried not to laugh.

Cruz tackle-hugged me and pressed me to my back before kissing me. I swore I could feel happiness bubbling from that kiss.

When we broke apart, I worried the inside of my jaw. "So, does that mean you want to ditch the condoms?"

Cruz tipped my chin and made my eyes meet his. "I want whatever you're the most comfortable with."

"I say we ditch them."

He smiled as his eyes shone with fiery desire.

My stomach chose that exact moment to indicate its displeasure at having not eaten since lunch.

"Let's get carry-out and then we've got all night," Cruz suggested.

"I need to shower, I had cats crawling all over me today."

"You got to volunteer for a while?" Cruz pulled on his shoes and grabbed his phone and wallet.

"Yeah, it was nice," I said as I followed him up the stairs.

"Leaving already?" Cooper asked as he stood in front of the fridge drinking a bottle of water.

"Running out to get some food and then we'll be back," I answered. "If that's okay?"

"Sure thing." Cooper gave us a wink. "I'm just hydrating before the big event."

We laughed and headed out the door.

We returned to the basement a short time later with our Chinese food and settled onto the couch.

"I want you to promise me something," I said around a bite of crab Rangoon.

"Anything," Cruz answered with zero hesitation.

"Anything?" I cocked my brow.

He shrugged. "I love you, I'll do whatever you need. Minus murder in most cases."

I smiled. "Promise me that we will stay aware and not let the other get lost. We'll support and love each other and if it seems like one of us is starting to be drowned by the relationship—not going out with friends, not having hobbies of our own, that type of thing—we'll call it out and help fix it."

Cruz nodded. "I can do that. But I need you to know that I want to spend time with you. I like doing things with you and being by your side, even if we're just with our friends."

"I know, I like that, too." I took a bite of egg roll. "I think it's just important to be aware."

"I can definitely agree to that."

We finished our meal and gathered the trash.

"Go take your shower, I'm going to run this to the outside trashcan so it doesn't stink the place up."

While Cruz was gone, I took advantage of the really nice basement bathroom. The idea that had been niggling at the back of my head for a while was set into full motion when I rummaged for some soap and found a two-pack of prep supplies.

Maybe I was assuming too much—at least we'd already had the condom discussion—but I planned to be fully prepared in case Cruz was on board with where I hoped the night would go.

When I exited the bathroom, a towel around my waist as I ran a smaller one through my hair, Cruz eyed me up and down and growled when he kissed me.

"Let me shower. I smell like the shop." He rushed into the bathroom.

I wondered if he'd notice the one remaining box I'd left in case he wanted to use it.

A bit later, after I'd pulled the couch into bed form and lit a couple candles Jesse and Cooper had sitting around, Cruz walked into the room in only a pair of black boxer briefs.

"I guess we need to add a two-pack of enemas to the grocery list to replace theirs. You think Bev would be okay with picking those up on her weekly trip?" Cruz teased and wrapped me in his arms.

I laughed. "Probably better pick those up on our own." I melted into his embrace, losing myself in his kiss, moaning against his tongue as it dipped and swept through my mouth.

"Whatdya want?" Cruz asked gruffly.

"Wanna be in you for the warm up." I bit my lip and tried not to grin when Cruz groaned.

"Warm up?"

"Yeah, gotta make sure everything is working

correctly. Then we'll move to the main event. Want you in me."

"You're sure?"

I nodded. "Never been more sure of anything."

Cruz tumbled us to the bed and I made short work of getting his underwear off.

"Lube's in the bathroom I think. Better put that on the list of replacements, too." Cruz stroked his thick cock as I dropped my towel and retrieved the bottle.

"I feel like we've missed out on so much time and there's so much I want to do," I settled between his legs and moaned when his hands clasped my ass and rubbed our cocks together.

"We've got the rest of our lives, Lo. No need to hurry. Just do what feels right." Cruz nuzzled my neck. "And feel free to entertain the old man with stories of all these things you want to do."

I chuckled. "Wanna bend you over the couch and fuck you. Wanna try shower sex. Want you on your hands and knees."

Cruz shut me up with a hard, deep kiss as he gripped my ass and pressed our leaking cocks together. "Go on," he panted against my lips.

"Wanna ride you. Want you between my legs, sliding into me so I can see your face. Want you to take me from behind while we're laying down."

"You been studying the Kama Sutra? Damn, you're killing me." Cruz sucked on my collarbone and smiled against my skin when I gasped and rolled my hips. "All the time in the world, we'll check each one off. Sounds like the perfect bucket list to me." Cruz cupped my face and kissed me long and slow, his slick tongue swirling with mine and sending heat through my veins. "Pick number one, your choice. Whatdya want?"

"Want you on your knees," I said. When Cruz complied, I nestled my cock between his ass cheeks and leaned forward to whisper. "Figure we better make use of this one sooner rather than later. Never know how those knees will age."

"Mouthy little shit," Cruz groused as he pressed his ass against my dick. "Get in me, wanna feel you. No prep, just in me."

I ignored his command, because of course I did, and slicked his hole with lube. After coating my shaft, I pressed my throbbing head against his entrance and pushed in slowly.

Between the super sexy noises coming from Cruz and the view I had of his body opening for me, I knew our warm-up would be done long before I was ready for it to be. My balls were already drawn tight and I couldn't fight the urge to grip his hips, thrusting hard and fast.

"Fuuuuck," Cruz moaned. "Just like that. So damn good."

I bent over his back and bit at his ear. "Wanna feel you come, feel you so tight on my cock." Wrapping an arm around his chest, I straightened up and pulled him with me, his back pressed against my chest as I continued to slide my dick deep. Keeping one arm around his chest, I reached for his cock and began to stroke.

"Fuck, Lo, I'm gonna come," Cruz panted as he reached behind and gripped my ass.

"Do it, come for me," I ordered.

With the first pulse of his dick in my hand and his head falling back against my shoulder, I knew Cruz was gone. As his ass clenched around my shaft, I thrust a final time and unloaded my release with a moan.

We collapsed on the bed and I was glad I'd thought to put a spare blanket down so we didn't ruin Jesse's couch or have to sleep in the wet spot.

"Holy fucking shit, that was amazing," Cruz mumbled. "Don't care if you never want to bottom because I could get use to that every damn day."

"Too bad, old man. You better recharge because that was just the warm-up, remember? You gave me permission to call the positions and the next one is me on my back taking that monster cock of yours."

My words wavered slightly, but not from nerves, only from desire and anticipation.

Taking a moment to clean up, we soon fell into bed to sleep until the main event.

A few hours later, I woke to kisses on my neck. "Mmmm, missed that," I murmured.

"Never again. Need you in my bed, in my arms. Always," Cruz whispered.

"You ready again? Or do your old bones need more time to recoup?" I teased.

Cruz pressed his rock-hard erection against my ass. "Anything feel old about that bone?"

I chuckled and pushed my ass back on him. "Touché."

"Plus, you're going to be twenty-one soon, so for a while there will only be fourteen years difference. I think that's not too much." Cruz trailed kisses along my jawline.

"I'd kinda forgotten about my birthday," I admitted, stretching to expose my neck to more kisses.

"I didn't. Hope you don't mind, but I've been making plans. Figured your twenty-first is kinda a big deal."

I gasped and rolled in his arms. "You're throwing me a party?"

Cruz kissed me. "Of course."

"When did you start planning it?"

He shrugged. "I don't know. I think I started talking to the crew about it like a month ago. Wanted to be sure they could come."

My eyes filled with tears. "I made us take a break and you were still planning to throw me a birthday party?"

"I told you, boyfriend or not, sex or not, you're the person I love the most in this world and of course I want to throw you a party."

We spent the next few minutes in a sloppy wet kiss of smiles, teeth, tears, and tongues. When we broke apart, my chest continued to heave as my heart beat a million miles a minute because of what this man meant to me. I fisted the back of his head and pulled him close so our lips barely touched. "Make love to me," I whispered.

Cruz held me tight, ravaging my mouth deeply, owning me completely. "God, Lo, yes. Want that so bad."

He moved just enough to grab the lube before settling back between my legs. I whimpered as the weight of his body pressed down on mine, our hot, hard cocks rutting together.

We kissed forever and I knew it would never be enough. Every point of contact between our bodies burned with fiery want. My entire being screamed for more, begging Cruz to take me, have me, fill me.

"Please, Cruz, I need you." I rocked my hips.

"You've got me, all night, all of forever," Cruz whispered against my lips. "But we're not rushing this. I don't want to hurt you."

"Then do what you need to do because I'm dying."

Cruz chuckled as he positioned our bodies the way he wanted them. With soft fingers and gentle kisses, he spread my ass, flicking at my hole with his tongue. He licked and swirled, spearing me and working my muscle open with each pass of that hot, wet, glorious tongue.

My cock begged for friction, but I knew the moment I touched myself, I'd be gone, so I gripped the sheets and gave in to Cruz's feast of my ass.

"Ready for a finger?"

"I'm ready for your cock." In reality, I knew Cruz was big and I likely needed more prep for comfort and safety, but I was dying.

"Patience. Do you want a finger?"

"Yessss," I whined.

Cruz lubed my ass and his fingers and began a long, torturous game of stretching me open all while teasing my gland with each and every deep slide into my body. I'd never fantasized much about edging, but Cruz turned out to be a master of bringing me close to release time and time again.

When I truly thought I'd shoot all over myself with or without his cock in my ass, I whimpered and begged, "Please. Please, Cruz. I need you inside me." My body was on fire, ready to burst, but heavy and relaxed from Cruz's drugging kisses and touch.

He finally, finally positioned himself between my knees. As he caressed my knees, I noticed his shaky hands. Sitting up, my legs around his as he knelt before me, I stilled his hands. I glanced up at him. "You okay?"

Cruz swallowed hard. "Just don't want to hurt you."

"You won't. I've been thoroughly prepped to within an inch of my life," I teased and leaned in to kiss him. "I want this. Want you."

Cruz captured my mouth with a deep groan and pushed me to my back, settling heavily between my spread legs. "Tell me if it's too much." He retreated just enough that he was able to grip the base of his cock and press his wide head against my waiting hole.

Torn between wanting to close my eyes and savor the moment versus watching Cruz, I gave in and kept my eyes trained on his face. I wanted him inside, wanted more than anything to feel that pleasure and complete our connection in the most intimate way. But watching his face, the love and awe that filled it as he took me was nearly overwhelming. His tight control never once wavered as he inched into me, I'd never felt more loved and protected.

The stinging stretch took my breath away, but Cruz shifted to bring our chests together and kissed me long and slow as my body adjusted to his invasion. When his tight balls pressed against my ass, Cruz paused and pressed his forehead against mine. "You okay?"

"I'm so good." I cupped his face, never taking my eyes from his. "You feel amazing, so right."

Cruz worked his arms under mine and held me close as he set a slow rhythm, thrusting deep, pulling out, and pumping into me again and again.

The fullness was intense and having Cruz in me, owning me, was a sensation I knew I'd quickly become addicted to. He'd worked me up so well and my cock throbbed between us, luxuriating in the friction of his body against mine.

"Fuck," Cruz bit out, "I'm not going to last long. You're too damn good."

"I'm so close." I reached between us to stroke my length, moaning at the touch.

Cruz increased the strength of his thrusts but

never broke the slow pace, driving me to the brink. With a swipe of my thumb over my leaking slit, I cried out, shooting my hot release just as Cruz gave a final thrust. He groaned as his orgasm washed over him, his cock pulsing inside me as he filled me with his load. My ass clenched around his thick shaft and I rode the high of my release as Cruz held me tightly.

When we finally returned to the planet, Cruz pulled from me slowly, both of us wincing at the loss. He wandered to the bathroom before returning to the bed with a wet cloth. He wiped us both clean and gathered me in his arms.

"I love you so damn much," he whispered. "That was more than I ever imagined it would be—and I've imagined a lot."

I smiled and cuddled into his chest before glancing up to stare into those gorgeous brown eyes. "I've imagined a lot, too, and I agree that the real thing totally went far past my fantasies. You were amazing." I kissed his chin before pulling him closer and devouring his mouth. "I love you. Thank you for giving me the space I needed. Thank you for loving me as I am and being patient with me."

"Always." Cruz held me close.

We fell asleep wrapped in each other's arms and I knew it was the first night of the rest of our lives.

I woke early the next morning, confused yet

sated. Glancing around, realizing I was in Jesse's basement, I noticed Cruz had blown out the candles at some point. When I shifted in his arms, he grumbled and held me tighter.

"I gotta pee," I told him and slipped from bed.

After using the bathroom, I opted for a quick teeth brushing to rid myself of morning breath. As I brushed, I scanned my body. My ass was way too sore for a repeat, but my cock was wide awake and begging for action.

Cruz found me a moment later, wrapping me in his arms and pressing his own morning wood against my ass. "Morning." His words were muffled against the crook of my neck. "How do you feel?"

I spit and rinsed, forever grateful to Jesse and Cooper for having a fully-stocked bathroom. "Gloriously sore." I wiggled my ass and smiled as he groaned. "Definitely can't take you again, but there are plenty of other options."

Cruz reached around me and grabbed the second unwrapped toothbrush. He brushed quickly before spinning me around and capturing my mouth in a kiss so warm, so promising, I nearly melted. "What options did you have in mind?"

"Well, I do recall mentioning shower sex. And here we are with a perfectly functional shower." I batted my lashes. "You want a round of bottoming for me in the shower while I check another one off my list?"

Cruz quickly turned on the water and we climbed in.

After washing, the shower quickly morphed into more recreation than function and I learned a few things. First, shower sex maybe isn't as hot as it's made out to be. It wasn't bad, it was just kinda awkward. Give me warm, soft, dry sheets any day. Two, Cruz was becoming a pro at bending over for me and I fucking loved it.

By the time we shut off the water and dragged our blissed-out selves from the bathroom, it was definitely time to head home. We cleaned up the basement, tossed the sheets and blankets into the washer, and gathered a small bag of trash before making our way up the stairs.

Thinking it was early and we'd need to sneak out, I yeeped when we opened the door to find the lights on, TV playing, and Hadley eating breakfast. Cooper and Jesse both smiled knowingly as my face turned six shades of red.

"Thanks for the basement," Cruz said and placed the key on the counter. "My old room is ready again so I'll be heading home." He winked and took my hand.

"Thanks for…" I paused, suddenly overwhelmed

with emotion at how much these men had helped me recently. "...well, just for everything." My voice cracked and Cruz kissed the side of my head.

When we got home, Bev met us at the door with a huge smile and insisted we eat breakfast before going about our day.

"Oh, Cruz, do you remember that thing we were discussing the other day?" Bev gave Cruz a pointed look.

He frowned but then seemed to realize what she was talking about. "Oh, yeah. I remember. Did you find out any details?"

"Well, funny you should ask. Seems what we were wanting was available sooner rather than later." Bev shot a look toward the stairs.

"Now? Oh, wow. Okay." Cruz suddenly looked excited and nervous. "So, yeah, thanks for your help with that."

"Not a problem at all. I liked the idea."

"What in the hell are you two blabbering on about?" I wiped my mouth and placed the napkin on my empty plate.

"Let's help clean up and then I'll tell you. Or show you." A crazy laugh bubbled from him.

A few moments later, we gave Bev hugs and she told us how happy she was to have both of us back home. Then we headed up the stairs.

"So, um, I wanted to wait until your actual birthday, but it seems the gifts I was looking for were available sooner." Cruz held the door and lifted my chin for a kiss. "I hope you like them."

He swung open the door and I walked into our room.

And found two kittens asleep on our bed.

I turned to Cruz with a yelp and clapped a hand over my mouth. "You got me kittens?"

"Well, Bev and I got you kittens. She's the one who was working with the shelter and she's the one who made sure no one in the house is allergic." Cruz glanced around the room. "And it looks like she's the one who got the litterbox and whatnot. We can go get more supplies later."

The kittens stretched and yawned, waking from their nap at our intrusion.

"Oh my God, these are the two I've been playing with at the shelter!" Tears filled my eyes as I sat on the bed and gathered the little floofies in my arms.

Cruz sat beside me. "You like?"

"I love." I leaned over and kissed him. "And I love you. Thank you." I paused. "Oh my God, I've never owned a pet. What if I can't handle it?"

"Pretty sure you've got a list of things you can do that proves you can handle anything you set your mind to." Cruz kissed me again and shrugged. "Plus, if you need help, I'm here. I love you and I plan on spending the rest of our lives proving to you just how much."

I sighed and leaned into him as the kittens snuggled on my lap.

Meeting Cruz had shown me I was worthy and capable of love, given me a family I thought I'd never have, and allowed me to see that I didn't need a man to survive. I smiled as Cruz kissed the side of my head and scratched a kitty ear.

Maybe I was perfectly capable on my own, but I sure as hell wanted Cruz by my side as we journeyed through this thing called life.

"I think I want to buy a car next week," Logan said as we were packing for our weekend trip. His birthday weekend trip. We were heading to Indianapolis with most of the crew to spend Friday and Saturday night and celebrate Logan's twenty-first. "You want to come with?"

Warm heat filling my chest as I recalled the intensity of taking Logan bare, I tossed a box of condoms back into the drawer, but grabbed a full bottle of lube and tucked it into my bag and waggled my brows at Logan's flushed cheeks. "Sure. I know a good place. Gotta go in knowing what you want and be prepared for…"

Logan shot me a look and I shut up.

"Sorry." I gave him a guilty smile. "Please continue."

Logan smirked. "Like I said, I want to go buy a car. I wanted to know if you wanted to come with me just because, not because I need your expert opinion or help. I've done my research and I know what I want. If I end up needing input, I'll ask."

"Sounds good. I'd be happy to come with you." I held up my hands. "Just as company and only offer my input if asked."

"Perfect." Logan zipped up his bag. "Now, tell me more about this bar we're going to."

"Well, Rai suggested it. I guess he got friendly with a nurse who came to speak to his cohort—his name is Gabe, I think. Anyway, this guy lives in Indy with his boyfriend and a big group of friends. One of the friends owns a bar called The Salty Lizard and Gabe was telling Rai about it. When Rai heard I wanted to plan a party, he called Gabe who then put me in touch with the owner, Bode Silver. Sounds like a great place. Gabe assured Rai it's an open and welcoming atmosphere with great food and drinks. We'll be there with the general public on Friday night and Bode let me rent the place for a couple hours in the early evening on Saturday before the bigger crowd will come in."

"You rented me a bar?" Logan pouted his lips and pretended to swoon. "So damn sweet. I have the best boyfriend ever. And where are we staying?"

"Well, Dalton and Gabby are just coming Friday night then they're going off on their own for the weekend. Khi and Dre agreed to come—which actually shocked the shit out of me—Dre is riding with Jesse and Cooper, Khi will be there on Saturday. You and I are staying in a little apartment above an art gallery. It's called the Silver and Gold Creative. I guess Bode has a twin brother, Benji, who owns the art gallery with his partner and they rent out the apartment above it."

"Oookaaay," Logan drawled. "I love the idea of just us in an apartment. What about everyone else?"

"Well, Bode and his husband, Sage, used to live above the bar, but they have a house now because they have kids. Anyway, it's a three-bedroom apartment and they rent it sort of like an AirBnB. They're letting us rent the rooms. Jesse and Cooper in one, Rai and Spencer in one, and Dre and Khi can duke it out on who gets the room and who gets the couch if needed." I was psyched we got such great rooms without having to do the whole hotel thing. "These apartments are right in the middle of a great part of Indy according to Gabe. Shops, restaurants, arcades."

"Sounds amazing." Logan frowned. "I probably can't drink more than a beer or two, probably make it a cider. I know it's lame for a twenty-one-year-old, but I don't want to mess with alcohol and my meds."

"Not a problem. Spencer doesn't drink either. I don't really know about Dre and Khi. And I know Rai usually opts for water. Jesse and I stick to beer. Cooper may be the only one who drinks more than a little, but he seems to have calmed a ton since opening the preschool. I don't think I've ever seen him more than buzzed."

"So, we're going to a bar and not drinking? We're a fun bunch."

I wrapped my arms around him and buried my face in his neck. "We're going to the big city," I chuckled because Indianapolis was big compared to Remington but not at all in comparison to Los Angeles or New York City, "to spend the weekend with friends and have fun eating, dancing, shopping, and laughing."

Logan kissed me and the quick peck morphed into long, slow glides of his tongue as I backed him against the door and rocked my hips against his.

"And sex? Right?" Logan asked. "Lots and lots of big city sex in our cute little apartment over the fancy art gallery?"

"Obviously." I kissed his cheek. "Come on, we need to hit the road. Want to get settled and to the bar before the crowd picks up. Bode said to try to be there by five if we wanted to get food orders in and have our pick of seating before the crowd starts to trickle in around seven. Tomorrow night, we'll have the place to ourselves from seven to nine."

"Anyone riding with us?"

"No, Dre is coming with Jesse and Cooper, but they aren't leaving until the preschool dismisses. Dalton and Gabby probably won't get there until seven. Rai and Spencer are going to follow us. Khi will drive on his own tomorrow."

We loaded my car and headed toward Indy. With music playing softly and a gorgeous fall day ahead of us, Logan and I chatted non-stop throughout the entire drive. When we got to Indianapolis, I followed the directions and parked out back of the Silver and Gold Creative like Bode had told me to.

The keycode worked perfectly and we took the back stairs up to a cute little apartment that had definitely been renovated not too long ago.

There was a welcome basket of fruit, pastries, tea and coffee, and a map of the area along with a handwritten note on the table.

Welcome Cruz and Logan!

Make yourselves at home. Everything in the kitchen and bathroom is free game. Head down the front stairs and check out the art gallery if you'd like. We suggest a walk along

Mass. Ave. before you pop into The Salty Lizard around 5:00. Text or call if you need <u>anything</u>.

Benji and Rhys

"Oh my God, that's so sweet. I kinda love them already," Logan gushed as he studied what looked to be original art on the card. "But I have one thing I think we should do that they forgot to mention."

I smirked, having a pretty good idea what he was thinking.

"Art and shopping sound great, really. But," Logan sauntered over and wrapped his arms around my neck, "I was thinking maybe we test out that gorgeous bed before we go sight-seeing."

"I like the way you think," I growled before kissing his neck and pushing him toward the bedroom.

"Oh wow, I don't know what it is, but it's amazing," Logan exclaimed when we walked into the bedroom and saw the large, colorful canvas on the wall.

I peered at a little card next to the canvas. "Well, shit. This particular piece was made when both artists covered themselves in paint and rolled around on the canvas."

Logan snickered. "I have a feeling I know what kind of rolling around they were doing."

I shoved him to the mattress and covered his body with mine. "The exact kind I plan on us doing?"

"Mmhm." Logan hummed into my mouth.

It was quite a while before we finally made it to the art gallery.

The entire weekend turned out perfect. The Salty Lizard was my new favorite bar and the whole crew vowed we'd be making trips to Indy more often.

Bode Silver and his husband, Sage, were some of the most personable and fun people I'd ever met. They were like a perfect match—completely opposite in almost every way, but it worked for them.

"See, there's a definite age difference between them and it doesn't seem to be an issue," Logan said as he cuddled under my arm on Saturday night while it was just our group in the bar.

Bode smirked and Sage grinned ear-to-ear.

"Oh, it used to be an issue," Sage said. "Bode was convinced it would never work. But I finally wore him down."

Bode rolled his eyes and pulled Sage in for a kiss. "My cousin, Kyson, is married to a man even older than him." He shrugged. "I've learned that age is just a number and don't even think about it anymore."

Cooper sighed. "Awww, see, I'm not the only one going after sexy silver foxes." He wiggled on Jesse's lap.

A bit later, we got to meet the whole Silver crew over drinks and dinner—and a delicious cake I'd ordered for Logan. Physical therapist Kyson and his motorcycle shop owner husband, Bay, stopped by for a visit, as did Benji and Rhys—the artists and owners of the gallery. As our private party was winding down, more friends of the Silvers came in. Chase, a bartender at The Salty Lizard, and his mechanic partner, Xan; Ty, a hairstylist, and his much older partner, Vic; and Gabe—Rai's nursing friend—with his mechanic boyfriend, Danny.

Their whole group meshed perfectly with our Remington crew and I had a feeling friendships would come from our weekend in the city.

Even Dre and Khi looked to be having fun—okay, so they were simultaneously avoiding each other and shooting daggers when they had to be around each other, but at least they were there. They'd spent the day with the whole crew as we wandered the city, found great food, and stopped by a fun arcade to play games. It was nice to see them relaxed with friends despite their still-very-obvious dislike of each other. I wondered if they'd ever be able to work out their differences—whatever they were.

The Remington party took up a whole corner section as the bar began to fill up. We planned to drink and visit for a while longer before going our separate ways. Brunch was on the agenda for Sunday before we headed home.

In the middle of Cooper telling a story about one of his preschoolers bringing a mouse to school, a double groan-turned-growl-of-frustration sounded from Dre and Khi.

I glanced over to see the two of them gripping their phones, glaring at the screens. If looks could kill.

"What?" Logan exclaimed. "What's wrong? Why do you both look like you want to punch concrete?"

Dre's eyes cut to Khi just as Khi gritted his teeth and shot an annoyed look to Dre.

"Text from the boss," Khi grumbled. "Gotta leave first thing in the morning. She wants a meeting."

"Same," Dre said as he typed a reply and shoved his phone back in his pocket. "Shit." He pinched the bridge of his nose. "I didn't drive."

Every eye at the table shot to Khi. He stared blankly around the circle until realization dawned. "Fucking hell," he mumbled. "Whatever. You can ride with me. But we're leaving on time and we're not talking. At all. I'm nothing more than your taxi."

Dre gave a nod and a quick thanks. "Well, since we need to leave so early, I'm going to head to bed." He gave Logan a hug and exited the bar.

"Same," Khi said once Dre was gone. "Who knows what kind of shit the boss has up her sleeve; it's always something. Better get some sleep." He told Logan happy birthday and thanked me for the invite.

"Always, man. You're family now."

Khi stared at me a moment before giving a brief scowly nod and walking away.

"I'd hate to be in that car tomorrow," Cooper whispered. "Awkward."

The whole table mumbled our agreement.

As the bar filled up, our little group dispersed until it was just me and Logan saying thank you and goodbye to Bode and Sage. We promised to visit Indy again and extended an invitation to Remington anytime our new friends wanted a weekend getaway outside of the city.

Once back at our little apartment above the gallery, Logan glanced over his shoulder as we climbed the stairs. "Like what you see?"

I smacked his ass. "Love it. Can't wait to own it."

"Who says you're doing the owning? Maybe I

plan on staking my own claim." Logan yelped and laughed when I growled and chased him toward the bedroom.

Tackling him to the mattress, I pulled him close, devouring his mouth. "We've got all night, plenty of time for both."

"All night, huh?"

"All night, every night, for the rest of our lives if I have anything to say about it," I murmured in his ear.

"I think I love that idea," Logan answered breathlessly as he stretched and offered me the sensitive skin of his neck.

"And I think I love you." I nibbled at his collarbone and tongued the spot when he gasped.

"I think you better prove it," Logan challenged as his hands gripped my ass.

So, I did.

Want more of the Remington Place crew? Look Yearn on your favorite book platform. Buying direct from the author is always an appreciated option https://payhip.com/ADEllisAuthor

Interested in getting to know the Silvers and their

friends? Check out the two related series: <u>Silver in the City</u> and <u>Forged in the City</u>.

The individual titles are:

Silver & Sage

Silver & Gold

Silver & Spice

Hearts Ablaze

Hearts Afire

Hearts Aflame

ALSO BY A.D. ELLIS

Find all of A.D. Ellis's books at https://books2read.com/ap/RWrrNx/AD-Ellis

The *Remington Place* series continues - Yearn (book 4) is a steamy, enemies-to-lovers, forced proximity M/M romance between two EMS workers who have hated each other for a decade.

Power Struggle is a steamy M/M, age-gap, forced proximity romance set in a small town. A twenty-year history, rival schools and jobs, and a hotel with only one bed make for a hot and heavy, sweet and sexy, HEA-guaranteed love story.

Take Me Home M/M age-gap, opposites-attract romance with plenty of steam and a scene that will make you appreciate camouflage and work boots

Let Love In M/M age-gap, forced proximity, dad's best friend, bisexual-awakening romance. Available on AUDIO!

Let Love Win M/M brother's best friend romance. Available on AUDIO!

Buried Secrets Romantic suspense stand-alone title. Available on AUDIO!

Silver in the City (3 books- meet the Silver crew you read about in Forged in the City) Available on AUDIO!

<u>Forged in the City</u> (3 books- a spin-off series from Silver in the City) Available on AUDIO

<u>The BJ Boys Series</u> (3 books, small town, big love) Available on AUDIO

<u>Forever Better Together</u> (friends to lovers) Available on AUDIO!

<u>His Reluctant Cowboy</u> (age gap, opposites attract, cowboy romance) Available on AUDIO!

<u>What Blooms Beneath</u> (LGBT Fantasy romance) Available on AUDIO!

<u>Sawyer</u>

(this was the first M/M I wrote and you may remember Sawyer and Luke being mentioned in <u>Barrett & Ivan</u> as well as in <u>Ryker & Gavin</u>)

～

ACKNOWLEDGMENTS

It's always so hard to write this part because I'm worried I'll forget someone without meaning to.

Readers- you are the reason I write. As long as you continue reading my stories, I'll continue writing them. Thank you for your support.

Bloggers- your support, reviews, and promotion are very much appreciated. Thank you!

My author buddies- I don't know that I could keep doing this without our brainstorm sessions, laughter, road trips, meals, wine, and friendship as my support.

Thank you to my alphas, betas, editors, proofreaders, and ARC readers! Your eyes and input are beyond important to me. Michael, Tenise, Anita, Sun Shiney, Jamie, Courtney, thank you for your first and second passes over my words—I'd be lost without my alphas and betas. And ALL of the fabulous ARC readers, THANK YOU for reading!

Brett and Gage- as usual, I doubt you even grasp how much your support, input, and friendship mean to me. This author journey has brought many wonderful things into my life, and you both are two of the BEST! I'm blessed to call you friends.

My family and friends- thank you for your love and support, always.

ABOUT THE AUTHOR

A.D. Ellis is an Indiana girl, born and raised. She spends much of her time in central Indiana as an instructional coach/teacher in the inner city of Indianapolis, being a mom to two amazing older teens, and wondering how she and her husband of almost two decades have managed to not drive each other insane. A lot of her time is also devoted to phone call avoidance and her hatred of cooking.

She loves chocolate, wine, pizza, and naps along with reading and writing romance. These loves don't leave much time for housework, much to the chagrin of her husband. Who would pick cleaning the house over a nap or a good book? She uses any extra time to increase her fluency in sarcasm.

Find all of A.D. Ellis's M/M romance at https://books2read.com/ap/RWrrNx/AD-Ellis

Sign up at http://www.subscribepage.com/ADEllisNewsMMRomance for a FREE male/male romance book.